GLADIAT

QUEST'S END

COLLECTION 5

GLADIATOR BOY

QUEST'S END

COLLECTION 5

Vs THE SCREAMING VOID
Vs THE CLONE WARRIORS
Vs THE ULTIMATE EVIL

DAVID GRIMSTONE

Hodder
Children's
Books

A division of Hachette Children's Books

A Catalogue record for this book is available from the British Library

ISBN: 978 1 444 92069 7

Typeset by Tony Fleetwood

Printed and bound by CPI Group (UK) Ltd, Croydon, CR0 4YY

The paper and board used in this paperback by Hodder Children's Books
are natural recyclable products made from wood grown in sustainable forests.
The manufacturing processes conform to the environmental regulations
of the country of origin.

Hodder Children's Books
a division of Hachette Children's Books
338 Euston Road, London NW1 3BH
An Hachette UK company

www.hachette.co.uk

CONTENTS

ANCIENT ITALY

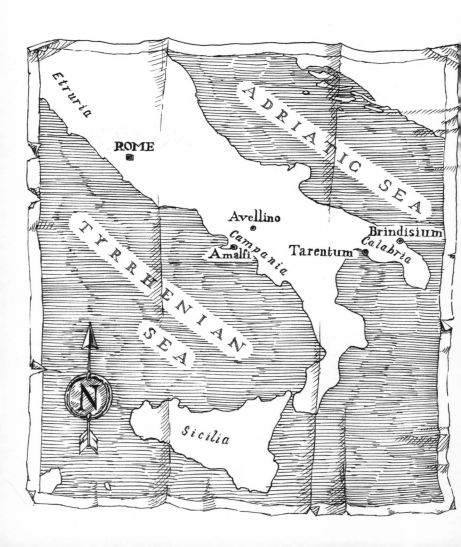

Vs THE SCREAMING VOID

*For Kim Tallulah Dance and the inhabitants of
Hoath.*

I would like to dedicate the entire Gladiator Boy *series
to Terry Pratchett. There is no writer, living or dead,
for whom I have greater respect. Thank you
for everything.*

CONTENTS

CHAPTER I

A DARK DISCOVERY

The soldiers erupted from the house, hauling their victims across a dusty path and into the small courtyard beyond it. There were only three of them, but they wore the dreaded armour of Slavious Doom's most feared guard unit and displayed the kind of confidence typical of the evil overlord's soldiery. Cackling like hyenas, they suddenly split up: two dragged the beaten man into the middle of the courtyard and forced him on to his knees, while their leader turned his attention to the man's sobbing wife.

'I will ask you one more time,' he said, as a large number of the terrified townsfolk gathered to watch the unfolding spectacle. 'Where . . . is your son?'

The woman could barely speak through her

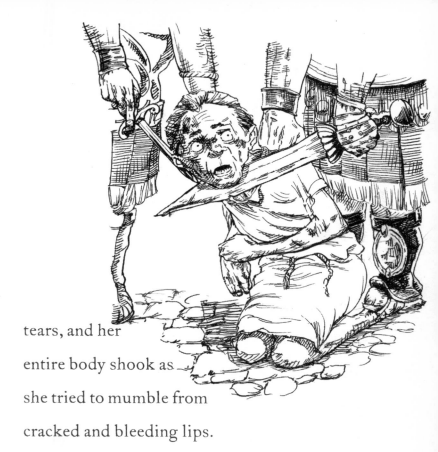

tears, and her
entire body shook as
she tried to mumble from
cracked and bleeding lips.

'Well,' said the leader, turning to his
companions. 'It seems the mother of Decimus
Rex is just as difficult to break as her boy. Hmm
… Captain Lich would not like this, not one bit.
We're going to have to cut off one of her

7

husband's hands – maybe that will jog her memory . . .'

As a rumble of mutterings moved through the crowd, the taller of the two guards holding Fenzo Rex drew his sword and snatched at the poor man's left wrist.

The woman screamed out, but the guard leader merely laughed at her.

'You see,' he growled, 'sometimes you have to—'

'I UNDERSTAND YOU'RE LOOKING FOR ME?'

The shout, which was infinitely closer to a bellow, seemed to erupt from all around the courtyard. The crowd instinctively glanced in random directions to find the source of the cry, but the guard leader, who had amazing

perception skills, gazed directly at the roof of
the house on the far side of the courtyard . . .
where a figure was standing on the roof.

'I AM DECIMUS REX,' it boomed.
'DEFEATER OF ARMIES AND
DESTROYER OF YOUR MASTER,
SLAVIOUS DOOM. YOU MAKE THE

MISTAKE OF ATTACKING MY PARENTS ON THE VERY DAY I RETURN TO THESE SHORES. A PITY FOR YOU.'

The guard leader squinted at the figure, which was partially obscured by the sunlight streaming all around it.

'So you're the great Decimus Rex?' he shouted. 'And what exactly are you going to do from up there?' He turned to his companions once again. 'He doesn't even have a spear! Hahaha! Hahaahaha!'

It was at this point that the crowd suddenly parted, but the guard leader took no notice. He was still staring intently at the roof opposite.

Gladius threw off the beggar's cloak he'd been wearing and erupted from the crowd like a rogue elephant, slamming into the head guard

with such
force that the
man hurtled
backwards,
crashing
into a pile
of logs
which
subsequently
collapsed on top of him.

The two guards holding
Fenzo Rex threw down
their captive and made
to intercept the attacker as he bore down on
their fallen leader, but they quickly found
themselves surrounded on all sides by a variety
of rough and ragged youths, all brandishing

swords with murderous intent.

'This battle is over,' Ruma snarled. 'If you think otherwise then let's see what you've got.'

'Take your injured master and hobble back to whatever hole you maggots crawled out of,' added Argon, as Olu and Teo both circled the group, warily, their blades at the ready.

The two soldiers charged.

Teo leapt aside to avoid the lunge of the taller man, while Argon swung his sword around in a wild arc and blocked the first three sword strikes he attempted. As the clash of steel echoed around the courtyard, Teo delivered two swift kicks to the small of the soldier's back, while Argon disarmed the man with a twist of his blade and employed a quick head-butt to stagger the man where he stood.

A little distance away, the shorter guard had run into a whirlwind of trouble with Olu and Ruma. The Etrurian attacked with such ferocity that he actually shattered the man's blade on impact, while Olu wrong-footed the guard with a series of well-placed strikes from a small but powerful mace he'd found aboard Tonino's boat.

Gladius watched with increasing delight as both soldiers suddenly lost their nerve, dropping their weapons and rushing to collect their fallen superior, who was weeping on the ground like a very young child with a bruised knee. The big slave grinned.

'Had enough?' he questioned, as the pair managed to lift their chief on to his feet. They were just hobbling away when Decimus arrived in the courtyard.

'Spread the word!' he exclaimed, waving his sword high in the air. 'Decimus Rex and his friends have defeated Slavious Doom and returned to the homeland. Slavers everywhere will learn to fear us!'

As a roar of grateful applause shook the crowd, Decimus fastened his eyes upon two people he had strongly suspected were gone from his life for ever: his mother and father. He ran to greet them, and the crowd slowly began to move away. They knew the difference between a public moment and a private one. The other slaves also stepped away, but Fenzo Rex beckoned for them all to enter the house, an offer which they gratefully accepted.

'We are so very proud of you, son.'

Decimus Rex's father, battered though he was, managed to fight back an ocean of tears as he looked down upon the son he had feared he would never see again. The boy's mother, on the other hand, could not contain her emotions, and was gripping the young gladiator as though she feared he would be snatched away from her even as they embraced.

Around the crude wooden table that served as the only piece of sizeable furniture in the Rex kitchen, sat the other slaves. Olu, Argon, Ruma, Gladius and Teo were all half-drowned with exhaustion: the journey from Pin Yon Rock had taken many days, and left the group feeling crushed in both body and spirit. Only Decimus held on to the determined expression that his friends had come to recognize as a sign of their leader's incredible willpower. While they all thought of returning to their homes and families, Decimus – it seemed – would not be content with his own homecoming until certain questions had been answered.

He broke away from his mother's all-engulfing bear hug, and immediately turned to his father.

'Slavious Doom is dead,' he muttered. 'His army lies in ruins all over Pin Yon Rock, and his henchmen and followers are defeated. But I must know, father: how are things here? Having seen what happened earlier, I'm guessing Doom's men haven't disappeared in his absence?'

Fenzo Rex took a long time to answer, aware as he was that every boy in the room now fixed him with an expectant stare.

'I'm afraid things are very bad, my boy,' he said, his face creased with worry. 'Your escape from Doom has given hope to slaves all over the lands, but I'm sorry to say that by killing the overlord you have merely severed one head from the hydra: Doom's men have acquired new leaders in his absence, and the slavery of children continues. If anything, son, it is far worse than it was before. Hundreds are missing, feared dead.'

'Who is leading Doom's men now?' Gladius asked, his big face contorted in horrified surprise. 'I mean, we've already seen the end of Drin Hain, King D'Tong and that hulking ogre, *Groach*; how many more apprentices can Doom have?'

'Rumour calls him the Mirror Master,' said Fenzo, gravely. 'I don't know if he was ever Doom's apprentice, but it is said that the overlord called upon him in times of crisis. According to what little the common people know, he dwells in a hidden fortress, deep in the mountains . . . but few have actually seen him.'

Decimus frowned. 'Then how . . .'

'He gives his orders through a soldier called Captain Lich; a terrible, black-hearted fiend who looks like death itself. He has sallow, sunken skin and is so painfully thin that many believe him to have already travelled beyond the grave . . . and back. He has a wooden splint in place of his right leg and only a single arm, yet he commands Doom's men with total savagery.'

'Enough of this!' The cry had come from

Decimus's mother, who now rounded on her husband with a fury in her eyes. 'The boy has not been back a day; we will feed him and his friends before they have no strength left to stand! Only *then* will I allow you to fill their heads with all your . . . dark news.'

A terrible silence descended on the room as, her eyes still brimming with tears, Decimus's mother set about finding food and water for her tired guests.

Eventually, their hunger satisfied and their thirst quenched, the boys' concerns resurfaced.

'You said hundreds had gone missing,' Olu prompted, as Argon and Ruma exchanged worried glances.

Fenzo nodded. 'Captain Lich snatched more than two hundred children from the coastal towns. He marched them west in two great snaking lines, all chained together like animals.'

Gladius risked a peek at Decimus, whose lips were already curled in a grimace.

'So what happened to them?' Ruma asked. 'They were headed to another arena?'

Fenzo shrugged. 'Everyone thought so... and then they simply disappeared. Two hundred children and the dozen or so men leading them; completely vanished.'

'No one vanishes,' said Decimus, shaking his head. 'Where exactly were they last seen?'

'A soldier heading back to Brindisi on leave reported seeing the group near the heartlands, not far from the Screaming Void.'

These words drew blank stares from Olu, Teo, Argon and Decimus, but both Ruma and Gladius looked up immediately.

'The Screaming Void?' they exclaimed, together.

Decimus looked from the pair to his father, and back. 'What's that?'

'It's a vast and treacherous chasm,' Fenzo continued, leaning back in his chair and shaking

his head, sadly. 'It's said to be deeper than the ocean, and local legend has it filled with the ghosts of poor souls who've made the unwise decision to try to find out whether or not that's true. It's called the Screaming Void, because often the last thing heard from those who venture too close to its edge is a tortured scream.'

Decimus took another mouthful of water, and gulped it down. 'Then that's where we start looking,' he muttered. 'A place that people *already* fear is the perfect place to hide stolen children.'

Every head in the room turned to face him.

'You are not getting involved!' his mother shrieked. 'You've been taken from me once, already, my boy – I cannot face the thought of losing you again!'

Decimus Rex got to his feet and looked at his parents with a mixture of love and regret.

'I am sorry, mother,' he said, slowly. 'But I will not stand by and see hundreds of other families suffer whilst I do nothing. My friends are free to return to their own homes, but I am going to find those captured children. If Doom couldn't stop me himself, then no minion of his will stand in my way.'

An infectious smile that started with Gladius travelled around the room.

'What do you say, boys?' Ruma intoned. 'One last mission, to avenge all those who fell under Doom's boot at Arena Primus?'

'I'm in,' said Olu.

'Me too,' Argon added.

Gladius's grin was threatening to consume his entire face. 'And me.'

'I come,' Teo said, his slight voice and speedy nod causing most of the others to laugh out loud.

Decimus folded his arms and grinned widely at his companions.

'Then may the gods smile on Captain Lich and his band of armed cowards,' he said. 'Because that snivelling wretch will need all the help he can get.' He turned to Fenzo. 'We're going to need a new set of swords, father; the very best you can get your hands on. We'll need rope, too – and probably some torches, if the legends about the Screaming Void are to be believed.'

Fenzo Rex stared proudly at his son, and

even managed a weak smile. 'Will there be anything else I can get you, boy? A warhorse, perhaps? A sailing ship?'

Decimus beamed back at him. 'Just talk to Gladius,' he muttered. 'If we need it, you can bet he'll think of it.'

CHAPTER
II

THE
IMPOSSIBLE
SIGHT

The group set out the next morning, following a crude map Fenzo Rex had drawn on a scrap of parchment. Despite this lack of clear direction, the route wasn't difficult to determine.

'It's just one straight road,' Gladius observed, peering at the map over Decimus's shoulder.

The young gladiator nodded. 'For the next few miles, at least,' he said.

'I hope we're in time to save them,' muttered Olu, eyeing the grim rain-clouds that gathered over the hills ahead of them.

Ruma and Argon were both quiet. The group had had a long discussion the night before, debating whether to get involved in another clash with Doom's evil army. Quite naturally, Olu and Teo had sided with Decimus: neither boy had close family in Italy, and both were being cared for by relatives instead of parents. Decimus insisted this fact made no difference to their decision to follow him, but Argon and Ruma felt differently. They both had parents who were desperately awaiting their return . . . and going off on yet another wild adventure would delay that moment considerably. In the end, they had agreed to rescue the other slaves and put an end to Doom's remaining disciples . . . once and for all.

Minutes turned into hours, and the group began to notice a souring of the land: trees that were usually lush and heavy with leaves at this time of year had become deformed and twisted husks, and a cold wind was ravaging the land.

As the group finally left the main road and headed through a thin, almost barren forest, they noticed that the once beautiful countryside was growing ever more depressing. It was almost as if a terrible sickness had blighted the land.

'It's Doom's men,' Gladius growled. 'When I was back in Arena Primus, I heard stories about them burning things: forests, villages, every type of landscape they passed through. It's as if they don't have the intelligence to do anything but destroy.'

The group walked on in silence for a time, none of them feeling the need to point out that the area they were passing through seemed cold and desolate, and mostly consisted of devastated ruins.

They had just climbed a rocky ridge when Gladius suddenly held up a hand to halt their progress.

'Wait! Is that Manduria down there?'

The group squinted at the distant settlement, and Decimus nodded. 'It must be – there are no other sizable towns on this map.'

Gladius shrugged. 'Then we must have passed the Screaming Void, already somehow . . .'

'What?' Argon exclaimed, his voice edged with humour. 'You're telling me we actually walked right past a place called the *Screaming Void*?'

Even Decimus smiled at this.

'Maybe it doesn't scream that loudly,' said Olu, as Teo and Ruma both laughed.

Only Gladius wasn't involved in the joke: he was staring behind him with a sudden, knowing look on his face.

'I saw it,' he muttered.

Decimus was still shaking with mirth. 'What did you say?'

'I actually looked right at it, earlier – just beyond the forest. I didn't realize what I was seeing! It's camouflaged, Decimus: the whole thing is completely covered over!'

The big slave turned on his heels and ran back along the path; the others quickly pulled themselves together and made to follow him.

Decimus gawped at the Screaming Void.

It was an impossible sight, when you finally understood what it was you were looking at: it was like a trick painting where things were not quite as they seemed. On first inspection, the entire expanse of land simply looked like the site of some terrible destruction. Hundreds of the spindly, crooked trees lay criss-crossed on the ground, covering an area so vast that it almost filled the view in every direction. It was only when you stared at the trees for a long time that you realized they were growing out of the ground *horizontally*, filling an enormous chasm that remained completely unseen due to the incredible net of decayed foliage that covered it.

'I can't even see a *gap*,' Decimus muttered. 'How would those soldiers ever have led two hundred children down there?'

'They went missing *around* here,' said Ruma, shaking his head. 'This might not be the actual spot where—'

'It *is*,' said Decimus, defiantly. 'ALL the trees around here are burned and damaged . . . apart from the ones covering this hole. It's a lair of some kind: I feel it in my bones.'

'At least we now know why they call it a *Void*,' said Gladius, evenly. 'I bet the space under that lot is enormous, and pitch dark: I bet there's not even a sliver of daylight.'

'We need to find a weak area,' Olu said, bravely stepping out on to a thick tree trunk and moving halfway along its length. 'There must be a place where the branches are thinner, surely.'

Decimus nodded, as the others began to edge their way on to the roof of the chasm. They each took a different direction, and spread out like a family of spiders on an enormous web.

'We need to be *careful*!' Gladius called. 'The further we get from the edge, the bigger the drop: that's just common sense.'

'So it would be really bad news if the weakest section turned out to be *right* in the middle?'

They all turned to Olu, who was crouching down at what would have been the very core of the chasm roof. The nervous smile he was sporting told the group everything they needed to know: a way in had been found, but it was an extremely perilous one.

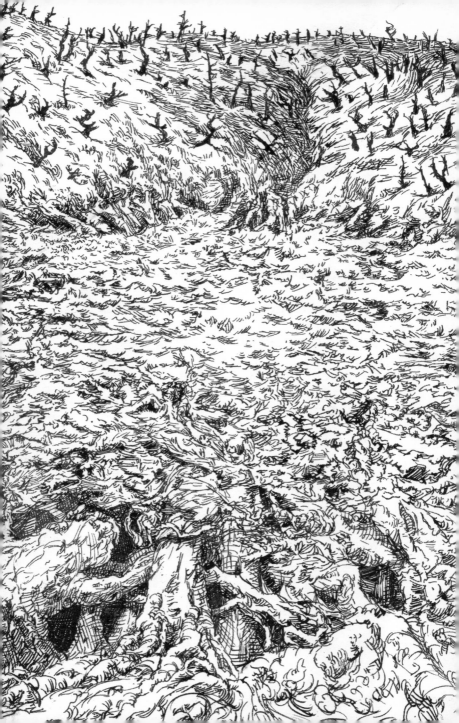

As the group gathered around the hub, Olu started to snap off twig-like branches and some of the weaker foliage that covered the area. In no time at all, a small hole had been made: Decimus reckoned it to be about the size of a cannonball.

'Let's make it bigger,' he said, reaching down and yanking away some extra branches. 'There's a heavy rock over by the edge of the tree line, and I want to drop it down there. We need to know how deep this chasm is.'

A few seconds later, Gladius and Argon both hauled the half-boulder towards the gap. Olu, Teo and Ruma helped them make the last few feet, while Decimus crouched low to the hole in preparation to listen to the resulting crash.

'One, two, three – now!'

The boulder slammed through the gap, snapping off several more branches as it plunged into the inky depths of the Void.

Decimus waited, almost holding his breath as second after second began to expire. Then he looked up at the others, who shared his increasing dismay.

'Nothing,' said Gladius, eventually. 'It's a long, long, *long* way down. The chasm must be absolutely huge.' He knelt down beside his friend, and ventured: 'I was thinking . . . that it might be an idea to burn it. If we do that, the sunlight will stream through . . .'

Decimus shook his head.

'No, I wouldn't do that,' he said. 'I know it's the quickest way in, Gladius, but we're not going to be just like them. Destruction is *their* way, not ours. Besides, if we create a massive fire and open up the chasm, it announces our arrival to whoever might be waiting for us down there. If the kidnappers are hiding out in the Void, I want our attack to be a complete surprise.'

Gladius clambered to his feet, and nodded. 'The rope it is, then,' he muttered. 'Does anyone fancy volunteering to go down first? I'll make a small fire for our torches.'

A short time later, Gladius and Argon had become firm anchors for the rope, their feet wedged into the stronger branches of the trees and their stomachs encircled by several layers of the thick line. Teo and Ruma both held fast to the rope in different places, ensuring that grips were clamped evenly along its length.

Finally, Olu crouched beside the hole, a torch raised above his head. He looked incredibly concerned.

'Surely four pairs of hands could support the weight of two of us . . .'

'I'll be fine,' Decimus said, picking up on his friend's worried tone. 'Just give me the torch and get them to lower me as slowly as possible. When I reach the ground, I'll tug three times on the rope. OK?'

Olu nodded, and muttered something under his breath. Then he handed the torch to his friend and signalled for the group to begin letting out the rope.

Slowly, Decimus disappeared into the gloom,

his torch sputtering above him as it threw up glimpses of the occasional rock formation and the outlines of decayed vegetation that invariably clung to every surface. The flames were conspiring with the dancing shadows to make the Void look even more menacing than it undoubtedly was. Decimus swirled the torch around him, trying to make out the edges of the world he now found himself being lowered into.

Above ground, Gladius and Argon were getting nervous. Being furthest from the hole, they were both eager to know what was happening, but the continued silence from Teo and Ruma suggested that even if Olu *could* see something, he wasn't letting on.

'Well?' said Argon, eventually. 'What's going on?'

Olu leaned over and peered into the hole. 'I don't know,' he said. 'He's too far down. I haven't seen him for a few minutes. I think I can still see a distant light that might be the torch, but . . . I'm not sure.'

A vague feeling of unease had settled on the group.

Olu looked up at Teo and Ruma. 'Do you think perhaps we should g—'

It happened so fast that no one really saw clearly *what* it was that had attacked Olu. One second, the young slave was crouched beside the hole, the next he was being dragged into it.

'Arghh! Help me! Arghghhh!'

Gladius and Argon instinctively rushed forward, but skidded to a halt as the rope in their grasp tightened and the recollection hit

them that Decimus was probably still dangling
from the end. They couldn't afford to move an
inch: it was all down to the others to save Olu.

Ruma and Teo hurtled forward in a mad panic.
Ruma stumbled and crashed through a network
of branches, embedding himself up to the waist.
Only Teo moved with enough speed, skidding

across to the edge of the hole and snatching hold of Olu's arms as the very darkness below seemed to consume him.

'Arghhhh!' Olu screamed, flailing wildly as Teo tightened his grip. The little slave tried to lock his feet in the branches, but he was pulled forward with such force that he had no time to work his way into the gaps. There was another, terrible cry from Olu, who actually disappeared into the Void, dragging Teo with him: only the little slave's legs were now visible outside the hole.

Argon spun around to face Gladius, his eyes wild with fear. 'Ruma's still trapped,' he spat, indicating the struggling Etrurian. 'Can you hold the rope if I try to help them?'

Gladius nodded, and Argon wriggled free of

the line, scrambling over the branch floor to snatch hold of Teo's legs. Screaming with the combined rage of fear and determination, Argon employed his savage strength to haul his friends back into the light. At first, it seemed the Gaul was making a futile struggle against an impossible foe, but slowly, very slowly, Argon began to win the fight. He heaved, and heaved, spit flying from the corners of his mouth and a thin film of sweat covering his brow.

First, there came Teo – moaning but still in one piece – and, finally, Olu. The thin slave was barely conscious as he was withdrawn from the Void, and his legs were covered with deep, bleeding gashes.

'He-lp me,' Olu managed, his last words before he passed out from the shock of the event.

A few feet away from where he lay, Ruma wriggled out of the collapsed section that had temporarily claimed his legs and dragged himself back on to the tree floor.

'Get Olu somewhere safe!' Gladius shouted, still bogged down with the weight of Decimus on the end of the rope. 'Ruma! Stay away from that hole! I'll pull Decimus back up!'

As the big slave moved backwards, slowly dragging the rope out of the hole, Argon and Teo lifted Olu between them and hurried him over to the edge of the tree floor. They had only just deposited Olu on the ground, however, when a frantic cry from Gladius drew their attention back to the middle of the hole.

'Argghh! It's taking Decimus! Quick! Hellllp!'

The coil of rope Gladius had earned with his retreating steps was beginning to unravel. Fast.

Ruma, who was closest to the big slave, barely had time to notice the coils vanishing before the rope was pulled taut and Gladius was suddenly wrenched forward. He collided with the Etrurian, and both were dragged, kicking and screaming, back to the edge of the hole.

While Teo tore up some ragged cloth from his tunic to tend to Olu's wounds, Argon thundered across the tree floor, leapt the gap that had previously claimed Ruma and dived on to the back of Gladius. Catching hold of the big slave's generous waist, he strained every muscle in the attempt to halt their forced progress. This time, however, the Gaul's efforts just weren't enough.

'Teo!' Argon screamed. 'Teo! Help us!'

The little slave abandoned Olu and flew across the chasm, moving with such speed that he was almost a blur, to the struggling line of slaves.

Thinking quickly, this time, Teo decided to wedge his feet into the tree network *before* he took hold of Argon's legs, giving him a greater platform from which to drag back the others. It might have worked, but no one could tell because, at that moment, the rope went completely slack.

Gladius flew back, crashing into Argon, Ruma and Teo as he cannoned away from the hole at a violent speed. All four of the slaves ended up in a crushing heap. As the stunned friends tried to regroup, Teo scrambled out from beneath the pile and hurried over to the rope. Snatching it up in both hands, he began to frantically haul it in. After a few seconds, he was joined by Argon, and together they retrieved the end of rope from the chasm of the Screaming Void.

It was covered in blood, and Decimus was gone.

CHAPTER III

THE MIRROR MASTER

Decimus awoke, cold.

At first, he thought he was alone and lying completely still. Then, as his senses brightened, he realized he was wrong on both counts. He was being carried along by a number of clammy hands, each sporting ragged fingernails that dug painfully into his flesh.

He tried to speak, but found that his mouth was stuffed with a cloth of some sort. He tried to struggle, but each time he did, more of the hands snaked out of the darkness and clamped hold of his limbs.

Realizing that resistance was, for the time being, a waste of his energy, Decimus relaxed, allowing his head to loll back as if he had fallen into unconsciousness once again. When he did this, he saw the torch he'd been carrying. It was

now being held aloft by an extremely ugly brute
of a man who looked exactly like the primitive
cave-dwellers he'd heard about when he'd
occasionally stopped to listen to the scholars in
the old town square. The man had a high, thick
forehead and walked with his mouth gaping
open, as if he was
permanently shocked
by everything
he saw.

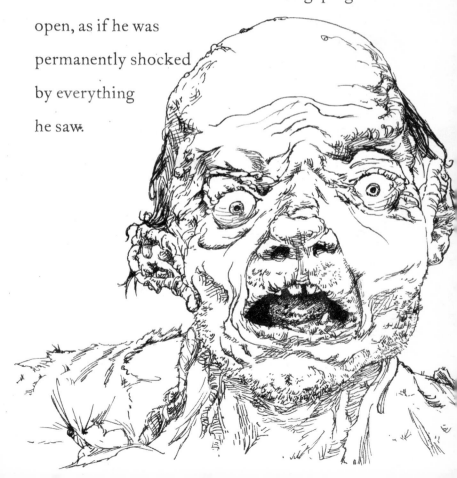

All around him Decimus could hear low grunts and growls, presumably uttered by the others who held on to him so tightly.

It had long been rumoured that wild men dwelt in the hills, tribes of forgotten warriors undisturbed by time and too primitive to be of interest to the Emperor. Judging by the strength of their grip, he reflected, they probably climbed up and down the chasm walls like spiders, waiting near the underside of the tree floor to snatch unsuspecting travellers who ventured too near their lair. If Slavious Doom's men *had* taken the children into the Void, they must have encountered these dark-dwellers or – worse – had managed to control and use the beasts for their evil purposes in some way.

The thought gave Decimus a second wind,

and he suddenly convulsed, kicking out with his arms and legs at the same time. This new attack seemingly took the tribe by surprise, and all the grips clamped around his legs were broken.

Springing back, Decimus slammed his head to the left, connecting with a skull so thick that the resulting blow actually blurred his vision for a second. It did, however, cause the beast holding his left arm to let go. He staggered slightly, then swung around and drove a fist into the face of the man on the opposite side of him. There was a low growl, but the grip remained tight and his captor threw a clumsy but powerful punch back at him. Rallying with exceptional speed, Decimus dodged aside and used the man's own momentum to catch him off guard, slamming an elbow under his jaw. There was another grunt, but this time it was followed by a dull thud as the man collapsed.

Decimus let out a relieved sigh, but as he prepared himself for a new assault the torch bearer suddenly padded forward with surprising agility and hit him square on the jaw. The strength behind the blow was such that it knocked Decimus sideways, and he collapsed, hanging by one arm from another tribesman who had reached out to grab him at precisely the right moment.

The torch bearer grunted, and the group hoisted Decimus into the air once again. Then they moved on.

Far above them, a few narrow beams of daylight had begun to peek through the chasm roof.

The glass fortress wasn't named as such because it was constructed entirely of glass, or because it had an unusual amount of windows set into the walls. On the contrary, the building was made almost entirely of stone and had fewer windows than most castles, having been built at the base of a dark and shadowy chasm. The glass fortress was, in fact, named for the incredible number of mirrors to be found within. They hung on every wall, covered every floor and were set in every ceiling, casting so many dim reflections that a single guard, upon visiting the fortress, could be forgiven for thinking that the place was packed solid, when, in fact, he was standing there alone.

It was a cold and terrifying place, but the Mirror Master liked it that way.

Slavious Doom's instructions had been very clear: if ever he was unable to continue his activities for any length of time, it would fall to his oldest and most trusted apprentice to succeed him. The Mirror Master had done just that, and with the help of the trusted Captain Lich, he had managed to cover the lands in a new darkness, bolstering Doom's slave army with children from towns as far north as Luna and Pisae. Of course, there was always the possibility that Doom might not return from his secret business in Yelang . . . but a sensible man would never count the overlord out.

A torch flickered at the end of the hall.

The Mirror Master swept back a lock of his

long, dark hair and allowed himself a smile. Even in a fortress full of misleading reflections, it was difficult not to recognize the approach of Andrus Lich.

The captain was bald, and his skin was stretched so tightly across his face that many thought him akin to an animated human skeleton. In fact, he was just painfully gaunt and thin, and no amount of eating seemed to change the fact. He had lost his left leg at a young age, while fighting a lion in the arena: it had been replaced by a wooden splint that clicked on the mirrored floor. His right arm had been claimed only a year later, this time by the snapping jaws of a crocodile. Life had been cruel to young Andrus Lich, but he had adapted by becoming crueller.

The Mirror Master covered his smile by

pretending to yawn.

'I thought I said I didn't want to be disturbed,' he said.

Captain Lich gave no apology, instead choosing to wipe a grimy hand across his lips.

'It's the cavers, Islaw,' he muttered.

'They've found a boy. They're bringing him here.'

The Mirror Master ignored Lich's use of his actual given name, and tried to focus on his words, instead.

'Can you not just put him on to the wall like all the others?'

Lich spat a wad of phlegm

on to the mirror at his feet, grossly distorting his own reflection. 'This one threw up a fight, Islaw. He even knocked out one o' the cavers . . . and we both know how difficult they are to put down.'

The Mirror Master nodded, and tapped his fingers on the corner of his ornate glass chair.

'Do you think he might be a good match for the Specials? They do need a worthy opponent in order to be properly tested . . . and none of the children we've tested so far have lasted longer than a few seconds with them.'

Lich sighed, and shrugged. 'There's six of the Specials, and only one of him: it wouldn't be much of a test.'

'He came here alone?' the Mirror Master prompted.

'Well, we don' know that,' admitted Lich.

'The cavers are always difficult to understan', but it appears there might 'ave been others with him that got away. So either our primitive friends are gettin' sloppy, or these others were jus' as feisty as the one they did catch.'

The Mirror Master smiled once again.

'In that case,' he said 'all we need to do is wait. Friendship is incredibly important to most children. You may find that—'

Suddenly the throne-room door burst open and a lone soldier came hurtling inside, stumbling slightly on the glass floor as he skidded to a halt.

Captain Lich spun around, and snatched hold of the man by his throat.

'What's your name, soldier? How dare y—'

'The cavers are going mental!' screamed the

guard, his face riddled with panic. 'They're running in every direction, and some of them are even attacking us! It's turning into chaos out there!'

The Mirror Master quickly rose up from his chair.

'I don't understand,' he snapped. 'What's happened, exactly? What has caused this?'

The soldier shook violently, locked as he was in Lich's terrible grasp.

'We're under attack, my lord! The chasm roof is on fire, and it's raining flames and burning wood! Someone is bringing down all hell upon us!'

Lich nodded, slightly, and then drove his head straight into the guard's skull. When the man collapsed in a heap on the mirrored floor, he turned back to his master.

'Pathetic maggot,' he muttered, prodding the guard with his boot. 'What's your orders, Islaw?'

The Mirror Master put his head on one side.

'Get the cavers under control using that *thing* they're all so terrified of,' he said. 'Then send all of the other guards to watch the children. We don't want a mass break-out. If it turns out that our latest captive's friends are responsible for this event, I want them caught quickly and brought before me.'

Lich nodded, curtly, and left the room. The Mirror Master waited for a few seconds, and then summoned another nameless minion from the depths of the fortress.

'Your wishes, my lord?'

'Send a garrison of my best troops to follow and assist Captain Lich. I sense he may have some trouble with these new intruders.'

'Anything else, my lord?'

The Mirror Master thought for a moment.

'Yes. Fetch the Specials from the vault.'

'At once, my lord. How many would you—'

'All of them,' answered the Mirror Master, with a demonic smile on his lips. 'Bring *ALL* of them.'

CHAPTER IV

FLAMES AND FURY

The slaves all gathered around Gladius, who was now standing at the foot of a bonfire that looked as though it might consume the entire landscape. Surprisingly, however, this particular fire was *sinking*, as the foliage and myriad trees supporting it began, very slowly, to collapse.

'I'm not sure this was your best ever plan,' Ruma protested. 'What if it spreads to what's left of the trees around us? We'll end up setting a fire from here to Tarentum!'

Gladius shook his head. 'It's already collapsing,' he said. 'In a few minutes, we should be able to see a way down.'

'What about Decimus?' said Olu, watching the dance of the flames. 'He's down there too, remember?'

Gladius rounded on him. 'Yeah, I remember you being grabbed too – and then whatever took Decimus leaving the rope covered in blood. Let's just take our chances and go with my idea, shall we?'

As Olu muttered a quiet reply under his breath, there was a thunderous roar and a large section of the tree floor collapsed, sending an incredible shower of sparks into the air.

Gladius began to circle the edge of the chasm immediately, running at a solid pace as more and more of the foliage fell inward. The inner depths of the Void were now being revealed: around the walls were hundreds and hundreds of cave-mouths, all opening into the cavern at various levels, and all surrounded by a network of sturdy-looking vines. Admittedly, many of these were now on fire.

'What are you doing?' Ruma shouted after
Gladius, his face a mask of fascinated
puzzlement.

'I'm looking for a path of some sort! A way
down on to the cavern
floor!'

The group hurried off after him, but they eventually arrived back at the same spot, severely deflated and gasping for breath.

'That's it, then,' said Argon, his shoulders sagging. 'There *is* no way down.'

Olu shook his head.

'There's no *path* down,' he corrected. 'We're going to have to climb down using the vines on the cavern walls.'

Argon rolled his eyes. 'Are you crazy? They're on fire! Look!'

'Not all of them,' Ruma observed. 'We can still get down – we just have to move fast. I have a feeling those *things* that grabbed Olu came from the caves, and I don't reckon we'd stand a chance if we got into a fight halfway down the side of the chasm!'

'Can't we use the rope?' Argon snapped.

'No use rope,' Teo muttered, his words attracting the attention of the entire group. 'If use rope, they get us all same time.'

'He's right.' Gladius nodded. 'We split up, and we use the vines. Now, come on! Let's move!'

The group scrambled to the lip of the chasm and swung themselves over the edge, using the vines to proceed down the covered walls as sunlight burst through the gloom all around them. It was a sight to stand and behold, but none of the group could afford to take that chance: their combined gazes were all keenly focused on the caves as they passed each one with great care.

Above and around them, pockets of fire

blazed in random patches, some dying away,
others flaring up. The entire chasm was bathed
in a pale orange light.

Argon was attacked first. The Gaul had made
the mistake of shifting his attention from the
caves for just a few seconds, and was peering
around to check if Gladius was making the
climb OK when a lumbering hulk sprang out of

the nearest opening and snatched him from the wall like a giant scooping up a child.

Several gasps went up around the chasm as Argon punched and kicked his assailant, driving fast and powerful strikes at the caver, who seemed to glance many of them aside.

The group looked on, powerless, as Argon and the immense beast struggled in the mouth of the cave, raining blows on each other in what was increasingly becoming a wild frenzy.

'Help him!' Gladius yelled, peering around the chasm to see who was closest. 'Teo! Can you get over there?'

The little slave immediately stopped climbing down and started to scramble *around* the walls, dodging several flaming branches as he went. He was halfway towards Argon's cave when an even larger foe exploded from the darkened hole beneath him and leapt on to the vines with a deafening roar.

Teo had the quickest reactions of the group. Even as the caver began to ascend towards him, he was already scuttling away at his top speed, moving over the vines as if he was simply crawling across the floor. The caver knew every single handhold in the wall section and sprang from place to place like the most skilled of hunters, but by the time he reached the vine where Teo *had* been, the little slave was almost at the roof of the cave containing Argon.

The cavers were now appearing from almost every opening, lunging at the group with murderous intent and howls of demented rage.

Olu was using his long legs to make several

dangerous jumps around the cavern walls, while Ruma had adopted the tactic of making for the nearest cave that appeared to be *unoccupied*.

Gladius knew he was the most vulnerable of the group. Bigger and slower than all of his friends, he would stand little chance of evading the emerging beasts if one made a determined scramble for him.

Reaching a decision, Gladius quickly drew his sword and slashed madly at the vine he was clinging to. Separated from the wall, it weakened, quickly losing its battle against the bulk of Gladius's considerable weight. The big slave flew into the chasm like a dart, screaming as he plummeted and holding on to the vine with every ounce of strength he possessed. He flew through smoke and fire, past cave after

cave and amidst a sea of hairy arms that snaked

out to grab him at each new depth he reached.

Fortunately, he was falling too fast to be easily

stopped and all attempts to halt his progress

failed miserably. At length, the vine began to

shudder as its lower roots were ripped from the

walls, slightly slowing Gladius's journey, but the end was still painful. The big slave crashed into the floor of the cavern, and cried out as a sudden wave of pain washed over him.

He tried to move, but the agony spread from his shoulder to his leg in one swift movement and all he managed was a weak slide on to his stomach.

Far above the struggling Gladius, Teo had joined Argon in his fight to escape the caver's attack. The little slave had leapt on to the beast's shaggy back, hammering a series of short chops into his neck while Argon delivered some of the heaviest and most powerful punches he'd ever summoned up. Not surprisingly, the caver was beginning to sag, folding under the pressure of the double attack ... but his companions were nearly at the cave mouth, scrambling over the vines like insects closing on their prey. Two of the brutes broke off from the main attack in order to go after Olu, who was still managing to evade even the stealthiest of the cavers.

Then it happened.

Olu made one jump too many, just as the vine he was leaping to caught fire.

'Arghghhh!'

The gangly slave dropped like a stone down a well, glancing off the wall in several places as he picked up speed.

'Olu! Noooo!'

Ruma moved without thinking, ripped a vine from the cavern wall and leapt after his friend. It was a brave gesture, but foolish – Olu was already too far down, and way beyond his reach.

The boy's despairing screams echoed all around the chasm walls.

Olu was snatched just as he fell past the last line of caves, by two pairs of heavy arms that half caught, half dragged him into the shadows. There was the briefest of struggles before poor Olu, still shocked and dazed by the fall, was bludgeoned into unconsciousness.

Teo and Argon were fighting a losing battle. Having finally overcome the heavy, mindless caver who had emerged to attack Argon, they were nevertheless beset by three more of the beasts as they attempted to climb back out of the hole. A quick rain of blows saw both slaves hanging limply in the arms of their overpowering enemies, and the cavers roared with delight.

The base of Ruma's vine snapped free from the

wall at the very last moment, leaving the Etrurian
with only the smallest of drops before he hit the
hard floor of
the chasm.
Ruma rolled
over as soon as
he met the
ground,
springing back
to his feet with
incredible
dexterity as he
peered up into
the gloom, trying see
what had become of
Olu.

'Ruma! He-lp!'

The Etrurian spun around to find Gladius slowly dragging himself across the dusty ground towards him. The big slave was bleeding from a head wound, and seemed to be struggling against great pain in order to stay conscious.

'Don't worry,' Ruma managed, hurrying over to his friend. 'I'll get you back on your feet in no t—'

'RUMA! BEHIND YOU!'

The Etrurian turned on his heel and was hit so hard that his entire body performed an involuntary somersault in mid-air. In all his many encounters with foes both large and terrible, Gladius had never seen such a punch.

Staring down at the Etrurian with a sick smile on his lips, Captain Lich spat a wad of phlegm into the dirt.

'I doubt 'e'll be wakin' up any time soon,' he growled. 'What about you, Fats? You got any fight left in you?' Resting on his splint, he brought a boot down firmly on Gladius's face and then repeated the move on his injured leg, prompting a tortured cry from the big slave. 'Hurts, doesn' it? We got your friend, you know – the one who came down first on the rope. How many more of you are there? Eight? Nine?'

Lich raised his leg splint and drove it into Gladius's damaged knee, twisted it at the last second to increase the pressure.

'Arghghghgh! Arghhghghghghghghghgh!'

'HOW MANY MORE OF YOU?'

'Five of us!' Gladius cried, his eyes streaming with tears. 'There's only five of us! Arghhhh!'

'You better be tellin' me the truth, Fats. I don' like liars. Only five o' you, eh? I reckon you're in BIG trouble, then. Big, BIG trouble.'

Captain Lich roared with laughter. Then he sniffed the air, and began to glance around him.

The cavers were emerging from crawl spaces dotted all over the lower walls of the chasm. Several of the larger members of the tribe carried the fallen slaves between them. Through his watery vision, Gladius saw Teo, Argon and Olu brought out and dumped unceremoniously on the ground next to Ruma.

Their prisoners deposited, the tribe then turned to Lich, advancing almost as if they intended to attack the gaunt soldier.

Lich grinned slyly and, reaching up with his single hand, he removed the heavy chain that hung around his neck. Positioned on the centre of the chain was a skull that looked marginally too small and misshapen to be that of a human.

'See this?' Lich muttered, peering down at Gladius with a blank expression. 'It's a dried monkey skull, nothin' more. The red glow comes from a tiny candle burnin' away in the middle. You wouldn' think such a thing would be so powerful, but you'd be wrong. These 'ere cavers are terrified o' it. They reckon whoever keeps the flame burnin' in this wretched thing is a livin' god, an' their lord 'n' master. As long as this flame flickers inside, they'll do ANYTHING I say.'

Lich held the glowing skull above him and all but one of the cavers bowed. The remaining tribe member, the largest and most muscular caver, stepped forward and nodded respectfully at Captain Lich, lowering himself on to one knee.

'Take these wastrels to the fortress an' dump 'em with their friend,' Lich commanded. 'Islaw will want to test 'em all against the Specials.'

The chief bowed his head and grunted an order at the rest of the tribe, who prepared to move off.

Lich wrenched Gladius on to his feet, suddenly aware that the big, wounded slave was mumbling softly under his breath.

'What's that? Somethin' to say, Fats? You want more pain? Is that it? Speak UP.'

'L-lucky and stupid,' Gladius managed.

Lich glared at him. ''Ey?'

'You're lu-lucky and st-stupid,' the big slave stammered, between cracked and bleeding lips.

'Is that right? And why would that be?'

Gladius turned one bloodshot eye on the captain. 'Lu-lucky because you found a way to control these m-monsters . . . and st-stupid because you just told me how you're doing it.'

Before Lich could muster the slightest offence, Gladius blew out a desperate lungful of air . . . and the candle inside the monkey skull flickered and died.

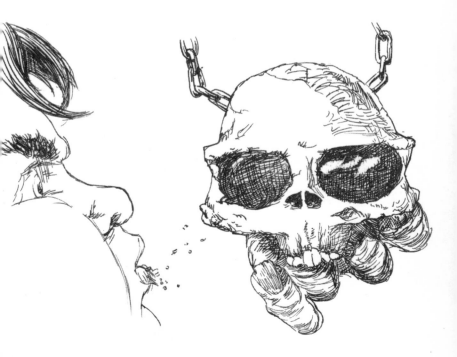

Lich gulped, the chief caver roared and the rest of the tribe erupted into a bellowing horde of chaos.

Vs THE CLONE WARRIORS

For Charlie James, who should never be called Charlotte to her face.

CONTENTS

CHAPTER
I

THE
BATTLE
OF THE
VOID

Captain Andrus Lich stood in the middle of a glowing pool of light cast by more than a hundred flaming torches. In one hand he held the battered and bleeding form of Gladius and in the other he held a deformed monkey skull that had, until recently, contained a burning candle. Now, the flame had been blown out . . . and with it had gone the power that Lich had used to enthral the cavers.

The beasts themselves, circling Captain Lich with a rebellious gleam flashing in their eyes, had abandoned their former captives and left the young slaves unconscious on the cavern floor.

Forming a greater circle around the cavers were the newly arrived soldiers of the Mirror Master's guard-army. Swords drawn, they

carefully moved in, eager to save their superior from attack but equally desperate not to start a fight they might not be able to win.

All eyes watched Captain Lich, and the big slave still struggling at his side.

'Stupid boy,' the captain snarled. 'Very, very stupid.'

Gladius licked his bloodied lips. 'I'd say it was smart – now you can't control them, can you?'

Captain Lich released his grip on Gladius, and belted the big slave hard in the face with a ragged fist.

Gladius collapsed, and the cavers moved nearer, their leader beginning to growl as the circle closed in.

Behind them, the outer group of soldiers also shifted towards the captain, slowly drawing swords as the beasts advanced for their master.

Seething in pain from Lich's strike, Gladius rolled over on the ground in front of the dread captain, and suddenly bellowed with all his might: 'CHARGE!'

The cavern exploded with frantic activity.

Certain the order had come from their master, the soldiers immediately flew at the cavers who – in their turn – took the cry as a challenge from Lich. They too lunged forward, and the chasm became a rioting, rampaging battleground.

Amidst the wreckage, Gladius forced himself on to all fours and attempted to scramble between the legs of the warring factions in order to reach his unconscious friends. However, he was trampled and kicked so often that he quickly found a fallen soldier and hunkered down beneath the unfortunate wretch, using his body as a shield of sorts.

Despite having only one working arm and a leg that was effectively no more than a wooden strut, Captain Lich was a devastating fighter. As the cavers charged in, he had drawn his own blade and set about them, spinning impossibly fast and carving his way through the horde without any sign of a controlled strategy. The rampaging soldier was a ball of wild energy, and his decrepit form had apparently done much to disguise the unyielding ferocity he fought with.

His crazed determination instilled the army of guards with a new confidence, and they no longer held back, crashing against the cavers in a storm of blades.

For their part, the primitive tribe fought only with their hands, but they possessed an almost limitless strength. In several places, cavers were actually snatching soldiers off their feet and *hurling* them into each other. Swords flew in every direction, some cast deliberately, some simply released in the whirlwind of combat.

Tortured screams, desperate cries and roars filled the chasm, which was living up to its name as a place of great and terrible suffering.

Then the tide began to turn.

In the end, the cavers were overwhelmed by the sheer numbers of the opposition. Peering out from beneath the crushed soldier, Gladius couldn't tell if the creatures had retreated or fallen in battle: one second the cavern was a tangled mess of furry backs and battered armour and the next it was just the glint of steel and lines of soldiers all standing in battle-ready positions.

Curse the gods, he thought. *That wiry old lunatic has won.*

He'd barely registered the observation when the dead soldier was heaved aside and he was dragged on to his feet.

Two rangy guards grimaced at him.

'Here's the fat one, Cap'n!'

Lich glared at Gladius across what remained of the battleground.

'Good. Now fetch the others and we'll take the lot o' 'em to Islaw.' He kicked the monkey skull into a dusty corner of the cavern. Then he limped over to Gladius and whispered into the big slave's ear. 'Your smart idea just backfired on you. Now those ignorant natives have fled, it's time for you to suffer . . . and believe me, boy, you and your friends *will* suffer.'

Decimus Rex was in a state of shock. He lay on a crude wooden platform, fighting back tears of anger and frustration as shadows danced from the torches outside his temporary prison. The last few hours had passed in a kind of tinted red blur. He remembered fighting the cavers, and being knocked unconscious during the struggle, but everything else was hazy at best. There were glimpses and images that filled in the gaps in his memory: being passed from the savage tribe to what appeared to be some sort of private army, a troop of guards flanking him and dragging him into a fortress of some kind . . . and now, this, a dank, dark cell of the sort he guessed he should be getting used to after the trials in the arena.

However, it wasn't any of these fractured images that had so stunned the young gladiator. The only image causing Decimus such intense mental torment was the one visible from the tiny window in his cell.

He hadn't noticed it at first, until the cries from beyond the western wall had alerted him. He'd quickly climbed atop the bench and pulled himself up to the small barred window in order to see where the noises were coming from.

And there, suspended on the cavern wall by chains that wrapped around their arms and legs, were rows and rows of children. The entire wall looked like a scene from some twisted nightmare. Each line had to contain at least ten to fifteen chained slaves, and there were more than twice that number counting down, leading Decimus to the conclusion that he was looking upon *all* of the missing children. They must have been herded together like animals, he thought, before being quite literally *hung* on the walls of the cavern. Many of them were obviously starving, their ribs clearly visible through their flesh and their faces gaunt and hopeless. They had been abandoned here, presumably after failing whatever sickly, horrific purpose they had been snatched to fulfil.

Decimus found a boiling anger begin to rise within him, but he knew he would have to wait until they came for him. Only then would he get the chance to right this terrible wrong.

A sudden clamour shook him from his

thoughts. In the corridor outside the cell, the sound of approaching footfall grew steadily louder and louder.

Decimus leapt to his feet and felt every muscle in his body tightening. Releasing a deep breath, he steadied himself for some sort of attack from his captors, but instead of that, the cell door flew open and several prisoners were shoved, kicked and, in one case, *flung* inside.

Ruma, Argon, Teo and Olu landed heavily on the floor of the cell, still barely conscious as they tried and failed to get to their feet. Exhaustion quickly claimed all but one of them. Only Gladius was wide awake, but the slave had evidently suffered a brutal beating on his way to the cells. His face was a patchwork of purple bruises, and his right eye was badly swollen.

'I think,' he managed, wincing as a network of pain coursed through his jaw, 'we found the ones responsible for snatching those children.'

Decimus nodded at his oldest friend and, without breaking eye contact, raised one arm and pointed at the cell window. 'I reckon you might be right, there,' he said.

Two hours later, the rest of the slaves were beginning to come around. By the looks of things, Gladius had taken the worst beating. Teo and Argon were both tired and a little battered, but otherwise unhurt. Ruma and Olu hadn't been quite as lucky, and both had sustained deep cuts and bruises in their various fights with the demented cavers. None of them were complaining, however, when Decimus showed them the horrible view from the cell window.

'We have to get out of here,' Gladius managed. 'I overheard the soldiers talking. This fortress *does* belong to the Mirror Master, and he's been using it to carry out some sort of sick experiment on the children.'

Decimus nodded.

'That doesn't surprise me,' he growled. 'I'm guessing the kids chained to the wall outside are the ones who didn't make it.'

Gladius shook his head.

'NOBODY made it,' he said. 'He does something to the children, puts them in a fight with some sort of terrible enemy. They ALL fell in combat, so they're all worthless to him.'

'Do you think he'll try the same thing with

us?' Olu hazarded, massaging his arms.

'You can bet on it.' Gladius nodded, vehemently. 'I'm thinking that's probably why they took our blood.'

The others took a second to hear the big slave's words, but Decimus looked up immediately.

'What did you say? They took your *blood*?'

Gladius pointed at the underside of his arm. 'And yours, I'm guessing. The only reason I know they did it is because I was *awake*.'

Argon, Ruma, Olu and Teo all quickly discovered similar wounds on their own arms. Even Decimus had one.

'Why would they take our blood?' Argon asked.

Ruma's face became a mask of sudden disgust. 'You're right,' he said. 'We need to get out of here before we find out the answer to that question.'

Even as they spoke in the shadows of the cell, the slaves' blood was being transported to the highest tower in the fortress. Captain Lich, leading a group of heavy-set guards, marched into the chamber and commanded one of the men to bring forward the brass container he'd been carrying. The instruction was obeyed, and the container was placed on the room's single great bench.

A door on the opposite side of the tower creaked open, admitting the lean, rangy form of the Mirror Master.

He crossed the room in three long strides and came to stand before the gathering.

'You have all the samples, I trust?'

Captain Lich nodded. 'Yes, Islaw. All kept sep'rate, like you asked.'

As if to indicate the truth of this statement, the burly soldier holding the container immediately forced it open, revealing six small compartments filled with an almost insignificant amount of red liquid. The Mirror Master nodded.

'Then we can proceed,' he said, turning to one of his own quiet servants. 'Bring out the Specials. Tell them . . . it's feeding time!'

The servant disappeared off into a narrow, sloping corridor that linked the east and west towers of the fortress. After a few minutes, he returned, leading a line of thin, unhealthy-looking youths. They all had sunken cheeks, watery eyes and teeth in various stages of decay. Their bones showed through their ragged clothing, and the flesh on their arms and legs was sallow, veins just visible beneath the surface.

The sight of them always made Lich feel slightly sick, but nothing compared to the revulsion he felt when they slowly began to transform. He shuddered as he looked upon them: only the gods knew what price Islaw had paid for the terrible, twisted ideas he had.

Slowly, one by one, the servants fed the Specials from the small, blood-filled containers. Then they were marched out of the tower and down to the Glass Arena.

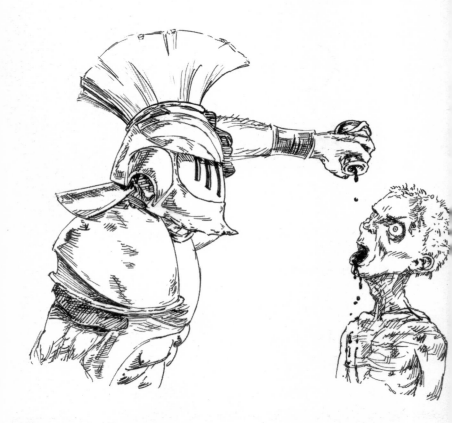

CHAPTER
II

THE
GLASS
ARENA

ecimus had planned it out a dozen times: when the guards came for him, he would work out a plan of attack. When his friends were brought in, that plan just got bigger inside his head. As it turned out, however, when the guards *did* come for them, there were simply too many of them for any plan to work.

They literally poured into the small cell, taking the boys in teams and dragging them bodily along a maze of corridors towards a destination unknown to them.

Decimus tried to struggle, but the five men holding him had positioned themselves in such a tight net that any attempt to escape was immediately rendered futile. The others were suffering the same problem.

At length, the group rounded a final bend in the last passage and were brought before an immense set of double-doors. One of the guards detached himself from the rest of the unit and employed a large iron key to unlock the doors before flinging them wide. The boys were then snatched up once again and literally hurled inside.

It took them several seconds to dust themselves off and check for any injuries sustained during the transport. However, their minds were very quickly otherwise occupied by the incredible sights all around them.

Gladius gasped, Olu felt his jaw drop, Teo just stared, wide-eyed and even Ruma and Argon were speechless.

It was Decimus who finally spoke, but he

said, simply: 'What IS this place?'

The hall they now found themselves in was a fashioned arena of sorts, but the oddest arena any of the group had ever seen.

The upper section of the hall supported a circular seating area that ran around the length of the room, but the lower section was composed entirely of mirrors.

Decimus glanced around him, noting the glass panels in every direction, even covering the back of the doors they had entered through. The floor contained no panels, however – instead, it was one vast mirror section all by itself.

There looked to be hundreds of boys in the centre of the room, but in fact, every aspect of the walls and the floor merely reflected the six boys in their various positions and attitudes. The result was deeply unsettling, and very confusing.

'I don't know why we're in here,' Gladius whispered. 'But I think it might be best if we focus on the ceiling, or on each other: anything but the walls . . . and the floor.'

Decimus nodded, but he found the sight

almost impossible to ignore. Argon, Ruma, Teo and Olu were all having the same problem. The view was completely captivating.

It was only when a grim shout from the gallery above echoed all around the hall that the boys were shaken from their trances.

A slender man with long blond hair and strange, delicately proportioned armour was staring down at them. His features were oddly beautiful, and for a second, even keen-eyed Ruma thought he was looking upon the face of a girl.

However, the cold and harsh voice – when it sounded once again – soon corrected that impression.

'My name is Islaw Danis. I am a servant of the great Slavious Doom, and I am known in these parts as the Mirror Master. Looking around, my young friends, I am sure you can see why.'

Decimus said nothing, merely regarded the man with a disgusted expression. All around him, the others were doing the same.

Before the man spoke again, he was joined on the balcony by the awkward and darkly familiar form of Captain Lich, who spat on the floor several times as he tried and failed to cough some lodged filth from his lungs.

The Mirror Master ignored the arrival of his companion, and instead motioned toward the arena floor with a thin finger.

'Today, you are honoured to be the latest part of my most important experiment. As my master, the great Slavious Doom, would say—'

'LATE.'

Decimus bellowed the word so loudly that it echoed around the arena long after his lips had stopped moving.

The Mirror Master took a single breath, and glared at him.

'Would you care to repeat that?' he said, his voice even.

Decimus grinned.

'You said the "great" Slavious Doom, twice. I just wanted to correct you. He's actually the LATE Slavious Doom. I killed him just off Pin Yon Rock; he fell into the ocean and drowned.' He took several steps away from the rest of the group, just in case his words brought further danger upon them. 'I'm sorry to be the one to break it to you, but your master's reign of terror is OVER.'

Gladius felt himself beginning to shake as his friend's bold statement concluded. Argon, Teo, Olu and Ruma all exchanged worried glances.

However, the Mirror Master merely smiled and gently began to clap his hands together in some form of mock applause. Even Captain Lich's taught expression was edged with grim amusement.

'I love your spirit, young man,' said the Mirror Master, with a deep sigh. 'This contest will be absolutely fascinating.' He moved to sit down on the bench above the gallery, and then hesitated, as if remembering something important.

'Oh, and I'm sorry to be the one to break it to

you, but we have a very special guest joining us for today's experiment. I would introduce you, but I think you've met somewhere before?'

The gallery door behind him was suddenly wrenched open, admitting two burly guards. The men were both well over six foot tall, but were dwarfed by the towering figure they escorted on to the gallery.

The winged demon-helm was gone, as was the golden armour, but even in silver plate-mail, the form of Slavious Doom was immediately recognizable.

Argon almost fell over backwards. Ruma, Olu and Teo moved closer to each other for mutual support. Gladius shook his head as if dislodging something that had flown into his eye.

Decimus opened and closed his mouth several times before he found his voice.

'Y-you're dead!' he cried. 'I forced you over the side of the ship! I *watched* you sink beneath the waves.'

Doom's mouth split into a terrible grin.

'Young fool,' he spat. 'Brave enough to destroy me, and stupid enough not to stay in order to check that the job was done. You left the remains of my men at Pin Yon Rock. They rescued me, and D'Tong's fastest ship saw me safely back where I belong. RIGHT HERE.'

Doom let out a deafening roar of a laugh which echoed all around the arena.

'Today, Decimus Rex,' he said, his voice filled with demonic mirth, 'I will watch the creations of my greatest apprentice reduce you and your friends to mere snivelling wrecks . . . and then I will pay a long overdue visit to your parents. You have caused me suffering and humiliation, boy, and in doing so you have forced me to make an example of *them*. They will be cast into the fires of Mount Vesuvius as a warning to other slaves, like yourself, who think to stand against me.'

A deadly silence settled on the arena floor. Everyone wanted to speak up for Decimus, who was now literally shaking with rage.

'You will not lay a *hand* on my parents,' Decimus thundered. 'If you do, I swear to the gods you will pay with your life.'

Doom smiled. 'So speaks the Chosen One! The one destined to retrieve the Blade of Fire! Oh, yes, but you failed – didn't you?

Hahahahahahaha!'

The overlord slapped his apprentice on the shoulder, and the Mirror Master quickly gestured to his servants. As the gathered minions of Slavious Doom took their seats, a slow, grinding noise filled the arena. It sounded as though a vast machine was working somewhere just out of sight.

Gladius immediately spotted the movement of the mirrors. Each great wall panel had become a revolving column, with identical mirrors on every side . . . so now, not only were the reflections multiplied, they were *moving*, too.

Argon leapt into a fighting stance, as if he half expected a rain of boiling rocks to be hurled on him from some unseen quarter. Olu,

Ruma and Teo all followed his example, quickly readying themselves for combat.

Only Decimus remained absolutely still, glaring up at the distant form of Slavious Doom with all-consuming hatred.

My parents, he thought. *I should never have left my parents. How could I have been so stupid … so arrogant?*

'Decimus!' Gladius yelled, realizing his friend hadn't even *seen* the walls start to rotate. 'Snap out of it! We need you here!'

When he got no reply from his friend, he marched up to him and slapped him hard on the back.

Decimus jumped, and instinctively raised his fists.

'I'm sorry,' Gladius muttered. 'But we've got problems – look!'

The walls were now moving at a slow but steady pace, spinning the many reflections into one incredible carousel of images.

It was at that very moment that the Specials

arrived in the hall. They stepped out from behind the spinning columns, creeping towards the group with careful, deliberate steps . . . and they might as well have been completely invisible, for none of the boys could see them.

'What is that long-haired idiot waiting for?' Olu shouted, peering around him in every direction.

'I don't like this,' Ruma growled. 'Something's wrong.'

Argon nodded. 'Why is nothing happening? I'd have expected wild animals or at least a rack of spikes by now.'

Decimus and Gladius were both circling each other, trying not to get too disorientated by the world of reflections spinning all around them.

Teo was a good head shorter than all his

friends, and had been focusing largely on his own reflection. Unobserved by the rest of the group, he stalked the nearest mirrored column, moving very slowly and watching his reflection move likewise. It was only when he was practically on top of the column that he noticed something very odd: his reflection was bleeding. A tiny trickle of blood ran from between Teo's lips and, on impulse, he raised a finger to wipe it away.

When he glanced down, however, there was no blood on his finger. Not even the tiniest spec.

He looked up again, and the reflection drove a fist straight into his face.

Teo flew into the air and crashed on to the glass floor, spinning around several times as the reflection leapt after him.

'What on earth?' Gladius grabbed Decimus and spun him around to face the unfolding situation, a situation that was difficult to see and practically impossible to believe.

The two Teos looked exactly the same, only they didn't: not really . . . not at all. The *reflections* of the two boys were identical, but the reality – difficult though it was to separate from the countless images all around them – was very different. The boy moved like Teo and was even, strangely, *shaped* like Teo . . . but he wasn't Teo.

As the observation hit home, Decimus immediately dashed over to help his friend, but was suddenly attacked by his own reflection and sent flying by a kick that slammed directly into the centre of his chest. He hadn't even seen the boy approach.

All around the hall, similar attacks were taking place. In one corner of the room, Olu found himself inside his *own* headlock. Argon and Ruma were trying and failing to avoid chops and strikes from *themselves*. Even Gladius found his path blocked by an equally large imitation, a kind of hollow-faced double

that drove a back-handed slap across his face with such force that his eyes streamed with water.

Up in the gallery, Doom was cackling with

evil laughter, while Lich smirked and the Mirror
Master looked incredibly satisfied with his
efforts.

Decimus tried to focus on his attack, ignoring
the many reflections that made it feel as though
was fighting twenty identical foes.

On top of everything else, the boy he was

fighting was
decidedly . . . weird.
He seemed to know
what Decimus would
do before he actually
did it. Every punch
was blocked, every
kick swept aside,
every chop countered
with a strike that

invariably left him injured and gasping for air. It wasn't that the boy was a brilliant fighter, more that he had the same *instincts* as Decimus. It was like playing a mind game . . . against yourself.

Decimus went for a desperate lunge, using all his strength to drive a double-handed chop at his opponent . . . but the boy anticipated his move perfectly, stepping aside at the last second and employing Decimus's own weight to flip him on to his back.

The young gladiator hit the glass floor with a thud, causing a network of hairline cracks to appear in the glass.

All over the arena, the group was being defeated.

Ruma tried everything to escape the headlock he found himself in, quickly resorting to a lift

which sent both himself and the other boy
crashing on to the glass floor. However, at the
last second he found the move reversed and the
boy actually landed on top of him, his elbow

firmly in Ruma's neck. The pain was excruciating, and made all the more difficult to take because Ruma remembered using the same move on several of his own opponents in the past.

Argon was being matched in both speed and strength. Always relying on his muscular arms to force any enemy to their knees, he resorted to a Roman knuckle lock, only to find himself rapidly losing. Legs bent slightly as he was forced down, Argon tried to dodge as the boy ducked under him and back-flipped him on to the floor. There was a crash, and the widening cracks in the glass doubled.

Olu and Teo, the fastest members of the group, were being outpaced.

Teo dodged every strike with his

customary agility, but seemed to find a rain of blows waiting for him *wherever* he landed. Realizing that he needed to treble his efforts, he went for a running kick that had never failed him in the past. Shockingly, however, the boy he was fighting met him in mid-air with the *same* move. They both slammed on to the floor, but Teo had taken the worst of the blow and found the wind completely knocked out of him. His opponent, by contrast, was back on his feet in seconds.

Olu's favourite method of attack was a leg sweep he'd perfected while training himself for the horrors of the arena. He performed the set-up for the move perfectly, driving a fist into the stomach of his opponent and following it up with a kick to the back of the ankles. Then, as his opponent flipped back on to his feet, he dropped to the floor and swept his legs around at an impossible speed.

The boy jumped. He actually *jumped* before Olu's feet reached the back of his legs. Moreover, he landed with a well-aimed fist in Olu's side. The gangly slave screamed in agony. It was exactly the move he would have done in the circumstances.

A short distance away, Gladius hit a wall mirror with such force that it shattered. He'd decided to use all his weight in a running attack on his opponent, but the clash had actually thrown *him* backwards. Glass exploded all around him, as one by one the mirrors all around the walls came crashing down like dominos. It cleared the view in every direction, but the sudden lack of confusion meant nothing.

Gladius was cut to ribbons, Olu writhed in agony, Teo was barely conscious, Ruma gasped for breath like a fish out of water, Argon was curled up, moaning loudly, and Decimus was trying and failing to get to his feet.

All around them, the Specials took up battle stances, but they had no one to fight.

The slaves had been soundly defeated. They were simply no match for the Mirror Master's strange and deadly warriors.

'Bravo!' Doom yelled, patting his grinning apprentice on the back and then clapping his hands together in a round of generous applause. 'At last we find the fighters who can beat these infuriating thorns in my side.'

The overlord rose to his feet.

'And now, my friends, I am afraid I have pressing business elsewhere. After all, young Decimus's parents will not throw themselves into the flames, now will they?' He turned to his apprentice and the smirking Captain Lich. 'Come with me. It's time we left this fetid hole you call a fortress.'

The Mirror Master glanced from the arena to Doom, and back again.

'What of the slaves, my lord?' he enquired. 'We have two hundred on the walls, outside, and these . . . unfortunates in here.'

Doom smiled down at Decimus and his defeated friends.

'Captain Lich and his guards can have the

pleasure of executing the ones on the walls,' he growled. 'And you can have your Specials finish these *insects*: their deaths are long overdue.'

As Doom and Lich headed out of the gallery, the Mirror Master gave one last command to his victorious creations.

'Finish them,' he said.

CHAPTER III

THE TIDE TURNS

Hope had faded for the group.

After so many victories, they now found themselves weary, sapped of energy by the sheer unthinking skill of their opponents.

Only Decimus had the will to carry on, struggling to his feet and expelling one last burst of energy in a rain of punches and kicks. Every single blow was countered and he was struck so hard by a wild, back-handed swing that his vision actually shimmered as he collapsed on to the glass.

The Specials moved silently around the group, each stalking their own prey. They were taking their time, watching for any attempts at sudden movement.

'It's no good,' Ruma shouted. 'They can

anticipate everything we do. It's over! We're finished!'

Gladius rolled on to his stomach, wiped some blood from his eyes and was about to prepare himself for the final assault when the boy before him came into sharp focus for the first time. He looked a little like Gladius, and moved *exactly* like Gladius . . . and, on reflection, it was practically impossible to outmanoeuvre *yourself*.

'Swap!' Gladius screamed, leaping to his feet and moving *away* from his own attacker. 'Everyone fight a *different* opponent.'

The group took a second to register Gladius's urgent message, but then – finally – the penny seemed to drop. They quickly scrambled to their feet.

Ruma leapfrogged prone companions and slammed into Decimus's Special. Teo took on Gladius's stalking opponent, while Olu flew into Argon's reflective enemy. The Gaul took on Ruma's leftover clone, while Decimus ploughed into Olu's likeness, leaving Gladius with the small and deadly character who'd been out-dodging Teo.

Suddenly, the one-sided combat in the hall exploded into a full-blown war.

Decimus knew all of Olu's weaknesses in combat. He'd watched his friend fight on countless occasions, and could ably predict most of the gangly slave's various methods of attack. The first punch was easily predictable: Decimus snatched hold of the Special's wrist and twisted it in several manic turns. Then he drove a knee into the boy's side and finished him off with an open-handed blow to the chin that had so much power behind it that it actually took the Special off his feet and turned him in a complete somersault.

The Olu imitation lost consciousness when he hit the glass, and Decimus saw a remarkable change come over the boy. Everything that was in any way *Olu*-like about the Special seemed to melt away, leaving a sick and pallid-looking youth lying on the floor, a few specks of blood around his lips.

Gladius had always wondered how he would ever deal with someone of Teo's speed and agility. The trick, he decided, was just to wait ... not to throw any effort into trying to keep up with the little Special. It soon paid off. Gladius threw a number of effortless punches which all flew wide of the mark. All the while, he watched how the boy jumped and darted around: left, right, up, down, leap, dodge, duck ... SLAM.

Gladius let rip with the most powerful punch he'd ever thrown, purely guessing where Teo's clone *would* be in the next blink of his eye. He was right. The big slave's meaty fist cannoned into the boy's face, knocking him out, cold.

The deflated, defeated clone hit the ground with a dull thud, sliding into a fractured part of the mirrored floor even as his skin sagged and the weight seemed to shrink from his arms and legs.

Argon snatched Ruma's Special off the ground and hurled him into the only remaining mirror column, sending out a shower of glass that flew in every direction. As the clone recovered from the collision and struggled to his feet, Gladius joined Argon and together they easily overpowered him.

Teo was easily outmanoeuvring Gladius's Special, but landing a solid blow on the boy was proving decidedly difficult, as his flesh seemed to absorb every determined strike the little slave made. In the end, he ducked two clumsy punches and leapt on to the larger boy's back, trying to apply a headlock while at the same time putting himself in a position where he could not easily be grappled. As he jumped and interlocked his arms around the clone's head, Decimus himself roared into the combat, slamming a series of single-handed blows into the boy's stomach. Working as a team, they forced the Gladius Special on to his knees and knocked the wind, and the consciousness, out of him.

As the group began to seriously overwhelm their formerly indestructible opponents, Ruma and the Decimus clone were fighting up a storm in the middle of the room.

Ruma was used to fighting Decimus. He'd chosen to take on his old friend's clone because he *knew* he was the only member of the group who had any chance of beating the young gladiator in combat.

Using every trick he'd learned in his real-life clashes with Decimus, he ducked and weaved with careful precision, allowing the clone's instinctive reflections of the young gladiator's confident attacks to trick him into making a mistake. Just like Decimus, the clone surged forward every time, roaring like a lion and throwing fast and furious punches. Unfortunately, he also possessed Decimus's single weakness: over-confidence. Ruma faked a dramatic reaction to a punch that hadn't actually done him that much damage. He pretended to stagger, half-dazed, and when the clone flew in to finish him off, he spun around and delivered an awe-inspiring high kick directly to the boy's jaw.

The Decimus clone genuinely staggered, and

Ruma finished him off with a plain and simple punch that he was certain would never have taken the *real* Decimus Rex off his feet.

The slaves staggered around for a few seconds, stumbling in the hall like a group of wounded, bewildered travellers moving through swampy ground.

'Th-thank the gods for you, my friend,' Decimus said, nodding at the big slave. 'Never stop thinking for us, will you?'

Gladius managed a weak grin, and shrugged. 'What do we do now?'

A dark look drifted into the eyes of Decimus Rex. 'I need to stop Doom killing my parents, and finish him once and for all ... but there's something else I need to do first.'

'Then what are we waiting for?' said Ruma,

determinedly. The scrawny Etrurian made to move off, but Decimus grabbed his arm and held him back.

'It's really important that you all do as I say,' he pressed, preparing himself for the inevitable argument. 'I need to leave right now, and I need to take Argon with me.'

'But—'

'Me?' The Gaul looked momentarily surprised. 'Why? What can I—'

'You're the strongest,' Decimus continued. 'And I'm going to need strength where I'm going. The rest of you . . .' he turned to face Gladius, Teo, Olu and Ruma, 'must free those children.'

Teo and Ruma shared a worried glance, but it was Olu – usually the most passive of the group

– who almost exploded with anger.

'Four of us against Lich and his army? That's insane, Decimus! It's suicide – even together we'd end up with a nightmare on our hands! Without you and Argon, what chance do we stand? All those children will die.'

Decimus swallowed a few times, but it was Gladius who spoke.

'Don't worry, Olu,' he said. 'We will get the children out – I know just how to do it.' The big slave turned to Decimus and patted his oldest friend on the back. 'You and Argon do what you need to save your parents, and we will come and find you when we've rescued the slaves on the wall.'

The group parted ways, Olu still muttering about *impossible tasks* and even Ruma and Teo looking unusually despondent. Only Gladius had a sly smile on his face, and it seemed he wasn't about to let the others in on his secret. He snatched a torch from a wall sconce outside the fortress, and made for the depths of the chasm.

CHAPTER IV

THE WALL

Captain Lich was employing his bizarre half-limping gait in order to stay ahead of the troop of soldiers he was leading. His wooden splint clicked on the cavern floor behind the fortress as the incredible sight of the prisoners came into view.

The cries of pain from the multitude of children chained to the rocks fell on deaf ears, as Lich ordered the soldiers to divide into two groups and sent them off in different directions, supplying each leader with a heavy set of iron keys.

'Use the footholds to climb each row to the top!' he shouted. 'Unlock one end of the chains and the whole line will collapse: they can all fall to their deaths. It's the quickest way.'

A bodyguard leaned over to mumble into his

superior's ragged ear. 'What about the ones on the lower rows, Cap'n?'

Lich shrugged. 'Just get rid o' 'em,' he said. 'I don' care 'ow it's done.'

The two sets of guards reached the footholds on each respective side of the cavern and began to climb their way up to the higher chain lines. Lich watched them with a mixture of excitement and annoyance. He'd always hated children, but he'd far rather have seen the boy's parents thrown into the volcano with the master himself. *This* was a job for the common grunts, not for a captain.

The two leading soldiers had reached the highest line of slaves. Ignoring the terrified, pleading cries of the children, the man on the right side of the line unhooked his keys and reached across to unlock the first chain. He put the key into the lock, took a deep breath and then prepared to undo the chains.

He didn't make it.

There was a sudden flashing blur, a deathly scream and the man was blasted from his footholds and sent plummeting to his death on the rock floor below. The keys rattled in the lock, but didn't fall after him.

Lich started in shock as, all over the cavern, the cavers appeared, swinging down on lengths of vine and springing from openings high up in the rock face. They were all screaming war cries and moving so fast that they looked like one giant mass of hair and muscle.

As they dropped from their perches and ploughed into the rest of the soldiers, Lich

staggered back and glanced around him for the
source of this new chaos.

There, at the back of the cavern, standing just
inside the shadows of the fortress, were four
members of the slave group from the Mirror
Hall ... and the fat one was carrying the

re-ignited monkey skull!

As he looked on, Teo and Ruma rushed forward, snaking around the dread captain and hurtling towards the wall.

'Kill 'em!' Lich screamed at the top of his voice, twisting around on his splint. 'Kill 'em all!' He limped closer to the base of the wall and screamed up at the soldiers still on the rock-face. 'Unlock that line! I want those wailing wretches dead!'

The guard now at the top of the line hastened up the last few footholds and took hold of the key, but he slipped and his fingers fumbled with the lock.

Teo darted up the wall like a spider monkey, taking the footholds two at a time. In the blink of an eye, he had scrambled over the backs of several soldiers and was now grappling with the leading guard, trying to headlock the man before he got a renewed grip on the keys.

Unfortunately, he couldn't quite wrestle the soldier's muscular arm down from the chain, and there was a sickening click as the key turned.

Thinking on his feet, Teo snatched at the unravelling line and quickly wrapped a length of it around the guard. The weight of the tumbling line dragged the man off the wall, taking Teo – still clinging fast – with him.

The chain collapsed, and twenty screaming children slid directly downwards in a catastrophic drop. However, Teo's quick thinking had saved their lives: the soldier at the end of the line hung mere feet from the ground,

his limp body forming a stopper that brought
all the children to a halt. They formed a
squashed line behind the man, as Teo moved off
his shoulders and attempted to unwrap the
chain.

All over the cavern, soldiers were clashing
with the enraged and vengeful
cavers . . . but this time the
battle was very
different. Spurred
on by their
flaming idol,
the cavers were
fighting with
renewed

determination and several flourishes that took the assembled soldiers completely by surprise.

Swords were drawn and lost as the swinging cavers flew over the heads of the soldiery, snatching the men from the ground and hurling them high into the air. Other members of the tribal clan simply dropped from the vines and crashed into random groups of soldiers, using their powerful limbs to pummel, crush and defeat their enemies.

Realizing that the battle was going against him, Lich drew his own sword and headed for the rocky crest where Gladius was still holding aloft the flaming monkey skull and screaming commands. He covered the distance between them in practically no time at all, and was just reaching up to dislodge the big slave from his lofty position when Olu cannoned into him. Lich flew backwards, his sword cast aside, and landed heavily with the gangly slave still on top of him.

Up on the far side of the wall, Ruma had wrestled the second set of keys from the other guard leader and was picking his way along the slave-line, assisted in places by the chained children who all cheered him on as he passed.

The cavers were winning the battle: their ambush had taken the guards completely by surprise. To add to their frustrations, Teo and the twenty slaves he'd freed from the top line had snatched up the swords of fallen soldiers and were weighing into the fray, the boys screaming with weeks of pent-up hatred and rage.

Gladius stood his ground on the rock, holding the fiery skull aloft with a nervous but determined look on his face: he knew he had to maintain firm command of the tribe, but was equally worried that Olu wouldn't be able to handle the dreaded Captain Lich alone.

As it turned out, he couldn't have been more right. Lich flipped Olu effortlessly over his head and, employing his sword as a support, forced himself back on to his feet. When the lanky slave leapt up again, Lich caught him a vicious swipe across the lower jaw. Olu staggered sideways, but Lich was only getting *started*. The captain put all the weight on his good leg, and drove the splint into the boy's midsection, finishing Olu off with an elbow to the jaw which sent the slave flying into a pile of jagged rocks. Never one to give a wounded opponent time to catch his breath, Lich crossed the path in a remarkably quick shamble, snatched hold of Olu's neck and yanked him back on to his feet, slamming a head-butt into the side of the gangly slave's face and knocking him off his feet once again.

Gladius watched the fight with mounting horror, increasingly aware that the cavers had nearly finished their assault on the army.

'Ruma!' he screamed, suddenly observing that the scrawny Etrurian had successfully retrieved the keys and was now climbing down to the bottom of the cavern wall. 'Help Olu! Quick!'

Ruma landed on his feet and peered around wildly, searching for his friend. When his eyes fixed on Lich, who was reaching down to snatch Olu up for a third time, he bolted across the path like a possessed animal, slamming into the captain with enough force to drive the hollow wretch off his feet. Lich scrabbled around in the dirt, but the wily Etrurian was characteristically relentless, and immediately drove two kicks pointedly into the older man's stomach. Lich rolled over and over on the dusty ground, then spotted the sword he had dropped during Olu's first attack. He gritted his teeth and made a frantic crawl to retrieve it. Ruma leapt over his head and landed on the blade, swiftly stamping on Lich's fingers when the captain tried to grab the pommel.

'Argh! You demonic little—'

The captain's words were cut short by his own sudden movement, a spinning, one-legged sweep which took Ruma by surprise and knocked him off his feet. Lich cackled with the

sheer glee of combat and smashed a fist into the
boy's knee, causing Ruma to cry out as he
scrambled away, trying to avoid any further
attacks.

Lich rolled over and clawed along the ground
after him, but suddenly stopped, his eyes bulging
in his head.

'Arghgghghghghghghghghghghghgh!'

He gasped, spat out a few strangled words
that made no sense whatsoever and, finally,
slumped forward, the life gone out of him.

Ruma, still moving along on his belly, peered behind him to see what had stopped the captain's eager pursuit.

Lich was lying face down in the dirt, his own sword driven hard into his back. Olu was still clutching the blade-handle, his lips twisted in a terrible grimace.

'You evil, black-hearted fiend,' he growled. 'Murder children, would you? Not now, you won't.' He relaxed his weight on the weapon and staggered back, offering a hand to Ruma who gladly took his friend's help.

The battle in the cavern was over. Still bellowing cries of well-earned victory, the cavers took care of the last few soldiers and then, following Gladius's equally booming commands, helped Teo to get the remaining slaves to safety. They crawled up and down the walls, seemingly clinging to the weakest and most insignificant of handholds, in order to put two, sometimes three children on to their backs in one attempt. Ruma and Teo unlocked every chain, manacle and leg-iron fixed to the mass of gathered children, while Gladius marched directly up to the enormous leader of the caver tribe.

'Here,' he said, thrusting the flaming monkey skull towards the behemoth. 'I believe this rightfully belongs to you.'

There was a moment of grim hesitation, before the caver understood . . . and eagerly took possession of the sacred relic.

Gladius bowed before him. 'We owe you thanks. May your gods protect you always.'

Then, as the tribe withdrew from the chasm, disappearing into various caves up and down the rocky walls of the cavern, Gladius turned to the newly-freed slaves with a tired but very relieved smile on his face. Ruma and Teo came to stand beside him, but Olu strode past the assembled group and climbed up on to the rock that Gladius had stood on to command the cavers.

'You are all free,' the gangly slave shouted, his voice echoing all around the rocks. 'And you will be as eager to return to your homes as we are!'

There was a roar of approval from the crowd, but when Olu raised a hand, his concerned expression soon provoked a hush of quiet. 'However, the leader of the group who came to rescue you is a boy called Decimus Rex, a great hero who is, even now, on his way to save his parents from your captor and his master, the evil Slavious Doom. I ask nothing more of you than to go free and live your lives, but for those of you who wish to stay with us and fight ... I would welcome your help to make every child in our great land FREE!'

For a moment, there was nothing but silence. Teo and Ruma swallowed, and even Gladius looked down at his feet.

Olu took two of the longest breaths he'd ever taken, searching the gathered army of slaves for anything that might pass as a sign that his words had been understood.

Then, a very small boy at the front of the crowd stepped forward and cried, simply:

'FREE!'

'FREE!' came another shout, and then the voices doubled.

Trebled.

Multiplied beyond measure.

Every voice in the cavern was unified.

'FREE!'

'FREE!'

'FREEEEEEEEEEEEEEEEEEEE!'

Far above the chasm of the Screaming Void and several miles from the forest that concealed it, Decimus and Argon managed to keep time with each other's fast pace. They crossed hills and valleys, past towns and settlements, and still they ran on.

'So we're not going to your parents' village?' the Gaul asked, his arms pumping the air as he sped along.

'There's no point,' Decimus breathed. 'Doom has a lead on us; he will take them prisoner and have them transported to Mount Vesuvius for their execution. It will take him time, of course . . . enough time for us to find something first.'

'And what's that, exactly?'

Decimus grinned as he ran. 'We're going to find the Blade of Fire,' he said.

Vs THE ULTIMATE EVIL

For Gabriel Coldwell, with thanks for all the help at Westwood!

CONTENTS

CHAPTER
I

THE
RETURN
TO
PRIMUS

'It's so much worse than I thought.' Decimus peered over the ridge and looked down at the valley that had once contained the dreaded Arena of Doom. Now, all that remained of the great and terrible building was a massive pile of rubble that stretched as far as the eye could see in every direction. From the way rocks were strewn around the edge of the valley, it looked as if the arena had mostly collapsed outwards, though Decimus could definitely remember wandering through the tunnels beneath, feeling as though the place was caving *in* above him.

'Look,' Argon whispered, pointing down at a wide and tall section of rubble that had presumably been the very centre of Arena Primus. 'Doom's men are *still* here.'

Sure enough, it was true. An entire legion of the overlord's soldiers was wading through the debris in one part of the ruin, while teams of guards in another shifted heavy blocks of stone into piles.

'Do you think they're rebuilding the place?' the Gaul continued. 'It certainly looks like there's some sort of mission to—'

'They're looking for the Blade of Fire,' said Decimus, a grim assurance in his voice. 'Doom still desperately wants it, and wouldn't forget about it just to get his revenge upon *me*.'

The young gladiator turned to his friend with a sly smile. 'They won't find it, though. When the Maw swallowed it and sank into the depths of the earth, a thousand tons of rubble collapsed on top of the thing. It's going to take them years even to get through the *top* layer.'

Argon frowned.

'Then how are we supposed to find it?' he ventured.

'Because we know something they don't. We walked no more than six or seven tunnels in order to get out before the arena collapsed.

Sure, they were steep and really difficult to get through . . . but we still survived, and when we emerged into daylight, we weren't anywhere near where they're digging.' Decimus turned slightly and pointed toward the far end of the valley, at a barely visible pile of outlying rubble. 'We were over there.'

Argon allowed his gaze to follow his friend's pointed finger, and beamed an equally sly smile. 'So we were!'

'Let's go.'

The two companions hurried around the top of the ridge and swiftly navigated the higher foothills that sloped down to the valley floor, picking their way carefully through clearings that might have been visible to the soldiers far below.

Staying out of sight in the lower hills, Decimus and Argon found their way to the outlying rubble in no time at all, and immediately began to shift some of the smaller rocks blocking a patch of ground that Decimus was sure covered the exit they'd come through on that fateful day, two years before.

An hour passed in the sweltering sunlight, but the heavy, exhausting labour bore no fruit . . . and still there were more rocks.

After a second hour, however, Argon suddenly hefted aside a massive rock and stopped dead.

'Here!' he said, almost jumping up and down with glee. 'There's a hole right here!'

Decimus joined his friend. Sure enough, there was an opening visible beneath the stones, just large enough to accommodate one of them at a time.

'What are we waiting for?' Argon said, wriggling down into the hole before Decimus could even muster a reply.

The young gladiator took one last glance toward the distant soldiers, and followed.

The tunnel was hot and impossibly dark,

with only a sliver of light from the hole to illuminate their passage.

'We're going to need a torch,' Argon muttered as he almost tripped over a stack of rocks that were blocking the path.

Decimus shook his head. 'No, we can't afford to waste any more time messing about,' he said. 'The Maw's cavern had a natural green light that swelled up from the beast itself. As soon as we get close we should be able to see . . . if it's still alive.'

Argon gasped in the darkness. 'You're not serious?' he muttered. 'How do you expect to find your way back to the cavern in the pitch dark? It's *impossible.*'

Decimus moved past the Gaul and patted his friend companionably on the shoulder.

'Nothing's impossible,' he said. 'Besides, I remember these tunnels from the escape. I don't know why; maybe, deep down, I had a feeling I'd be back here, someday. Hell, maybe the prophecy *is* right.'

He marched on ahead, leaving Argon walking despondently after him.

Gladius reached the lip of the track he'd been following and held up a large, podgy hand. The mass of former slaves gathered behind him suddenly shuffled to a halt, but this happened slowly, as the various other groups led by Teo, Olu and Ruma also came to a standstill. They were all armed with swords stolen from the Mirror Master's subterranean fortress, so the general slowing of their progress was anything but silent.

Ruma, always one to question any decision he hadn't actually made himself, hurried up to the big slave to see what was going on.

'Gladius,' he said briskly, noticing they were now looking out over a broad spread of what passed in the region for country farmland. 'Why have we stopped?'

'We're getting too close.'

'To Doom? Surely that's a good thing!'

Gladius shook his head.

'We don't want a confrontation before he gets to the mountain. Decimus should be the first to—'

'Are you mad?' Olu, who had been approaching and had overheard the conversation, looked shocked. 'Surely we want to stop him from ever *reaching* Mount Vesuvius? Are we planning to wait until Decimus's mum and dad are actually thrown into the volcano before we attack?'

The big slave sighed.

'Of course not, but we don't want to waste our only chance to defeat Doom and his army. Don't forget the Mirror Master is *with* him, and he's supposed to be a genius, right? I seriously doubt we can defeat Doom, all his men *and* the Mirror Master without Decimus and Argon behind us.'

Ruma looked suddenly disgusted.

'We have an entire *army*,' he whined.

'Exactly,' said Gladius, nodding. 'And we don't want to waste them by sacrificing them on

the altar of our *own* stupidity. So we
should continue to follow Doom *at a*
steady pace until we reach the
volcano. If Decimus *still*
hasn't shown up by then,

we make our move. Agreed?'

Ruma and Olu paused for a moment, and
then both gave a reluctant nod.

Finally, Teo arrived beside the group.

'What I miss?' he said, causing the others to
burst out laughing.

Decimus was feeling his way along the tunnel system in total darkness, edging forward so carefully that anyone capable of observing him would have thought he was on the edge of a cliff. Argon followed along behind him, listening for the sound of his voice.

So far, they had encountered and removed three different obstructions, all of collapsed stone and all blocking the tunnel from floor to ceiling. Two had taken mere minutes to shift, but the last one had drained the pair of both time and effort. Now, they were both fairly exhausted.

'It's not much further until this tunnel hits a junction,' Decimus assured his friend, as the floor suddenly sloped at a sharp angle.

'I still can't understand how you remember this place so well,' Argon mumbled. 'It was all a blur to me; we were running *so* fast.'

'This way.' Decimus continued along the passage, before his voice suddenly changed and seemed to come from another direction. 'I've gone right at the divide – try to feel the breeze on your face – it's coming from the main cavern.'

Argon followed, sliding around the bend in the passage.

Down.

Down.

Dowwwwn.

After what felt like an age, Argon began to notice Decimus's bold outline up ahead of him. The revealed sight could mean only one thing – the glow from the Maw was still alight, and reached this far into the complex. It would be easier from here on in.

'I don't understand why we can't hear anything,' Decimus observed, quickening his pace. 'I remember that roar as if it started inside my own ears.'

Argon shrugged. 'Maybe it's sleeping.'

'We can hope.'

The glow was now clearly visible, a greenish wash that seemed to shift and travel over the tunnel roof as though in some bizarre dance of light.

The two boys doubled their efforts, sprinting along each new tunnel with renewed determination. As they proceeded deeper and deeper into the subterranean network, the glowing light grew stronger and stronger, developing from a wash to an all-out beam of emerald intensity.

At length, Decimus rounded one final bend in the last passage, and skidded to an unexpected and rather abrupt halt.

Argon cannoned into him, and the pair almost tumbled down the collapsed underground canyon that now spread out before them.

'Look!' Decimus gasped. 'In the name of the gods – it's even bigger than I remembered!'

Argon said nothing: he couldn't agree with his friend more, but his mouth simply refused to open.

Ahead of them and far below was a vast, meandering crack in the earth. Above ground, it would have looked like a vast chasm,

impossibly deep and unthinkably wide. Here, however, it just looked like a gap in the floor, or a crack in a line of plaster.

The main reason for this was the Maw, an octopus-like beast so far beyond size as to be almost unimaginable. It was half in and half out of the gap, like a bloated spider hiding inside a wall-crevice with only its legs spilling out above the surface.

Decimus swallowed, suddenly realizing the enormous task ahead of him. Currently, the hideous expanse of the Maw's countless eyes was nowhere to be seen, presumably because the beast was either dead or sleeping. Decimus suspected the latter, as a terrible shuddering rhythm suggested it was not only alive but still, inconceivably, well.

'I thought you killed it!' Argon whispered in his ear, finally finding a shaky voice in the horrible cavern.

Decimus shook his head. 'I knew it wasn't dead,' he muttered. 'I'm just shocked it survived the collapse so . . . well . . . intact. Now listen to me, Argon – I need you to climb up to that top ridge and start screaming, as loud as you can for as *long* as you can. When the beast awakes and starts extending its tentacles, you're going to need to run *around* the ridge, avoiding them. I chose you to come with me because you're the only one strong enough to have a chance of breaking free if it *does* get hold of you. Now, did you get all that?'

Argon nodded, but looked momentarily puzzled. 'What are you going to be doing, exactly?'

Decimus grinned. 'Don't ask!'

He edged forward slightly, holding on to the rocks at either side of the tunnel mouth.

'Well,' he whispered. 'Here goes nothing.'

With that, he slid down the wall to the valley floor, and began sneaking carefully towards the sleeping monster.

CHAPTER
II

INTO
THE
MAW

Slavious Doom felt the approach of his apprentice even before the man drew near to him. There was something ever so slightly uncomfortable about Islaw Danis, the man who preferred himself to be called the Mirror Master.

'Is there a problem?' Doom asked, before the long-haired warrior had even announced his presence.

If Danis jumped even slightly, he did not show it. Instead, he glanced over his shoulder at the long line of soldiers . . . and at the two slaves they were dragging in their wake.

'Not a problem exactly, my lord,' said Danis, edging closer still and lowering his voice. 'Rex's parents are being given water every few hours, so all is fine there. We should reach the volcano in a little under two hours, in fact.'

Doom raised a dark eyebrow. 'Well then? To what do I owe your sudden company?'

His apprentice paused again, as if he was frightened to make any further comment. Then, very suddenly, his confidence seemed to increase.

'I wonder about the wisdom of the decision you made back at the fortress, my lord.'

'Oh?' Doom smiled to himself: he'd predicted this exact conversation.

'Well, it's just that if Decimus Rex is such a powerful warrior – was it entirely, um, sensible to leave him and his companions to fight the Specials *unobserved*? I mean, I have every faith in my creations, but it's just on the edge of possibility that . . .'

'. . . that Decimus and his friends overcame them and escaped?'

Doom turned his great head slightly and his eyes narrowed to mere slits. 'And then overcame the vile Captain Lich and his men, releasing all the child slaves from the wall at the same time?'

The Mirror Master was speechless. All he

managed was a weak and trembling nod.

'I expect you are right,' Doom finished. 'And that even now those pathetic rascals are building an army in the hope of saving that pair of ageing peasants behind me?'

The Mirror Master finally found his voice.

'Y-yes, my lord – but if . . .'

'. . . if I know all this, why am I doing nothing? It's really quite simple.' Doom cackled as he strode along. 'Decimus Rex will not come after me unarmed, not this time – he knows I survived his last attack and will never again underestimate my strength. No, in order to save his parents, he will take his new army in search of the one thing he thinks he needs in order to defeat me.'

A sudden realization dawned on the Mirror

Master's stunned face.

'The Blade of Fire!' he exclaimed.

'Exactly.' Doom turned to his apprentice with an evil, knowing smile. 'And I would hazard a guess that, even as we speak, my young friend and his horde of young warriors are doing everything they can to get it back . . . *exactly* as I had planned. Relax, Islaw – it will take Decimus and his army *many* days to reach us . . . and be assured that we will be ready for them when they do.'

The Mirror Master grinned at the overlord's intricate plan, but he couldn't help but feel slightly uneasy: *he was secretly quite certain that they were being closely followed.*

Argon could feel his heart pounding in his chest. Every muscle straining with effort, he dragged himself over the edge of the ridge and on to the narrow, circular path that ran around the boundary of the cavern roof.

Leaping to his feet, Argon peered down at the distant floor, trying to see where Decimus had gone . . . but there was no sign of his friend.

Swallowing a few times and trying to stop himself shaking, Argon took a deep breath and held it for several seconds. Then he let out the most powerful, booming yell he'd ever uttered.

The high-pitched cry echoed all around the cavern, bouncing from every crevice in the pitted roof and gathering more reverberations even as it died away.

Down in the base of the cavern, the Maw

twitched so thunderously that a great column of rock collapsed as the tentacles flashed back and forth. The great, jet black, slime-encrusted body of the beast began to emerge from its hole, looking even more like a fat and hairy spider as the tentacles dragged its bulk upwards. All at once, the many and gelatinous eyes of the *thing* sprang open in a terrible glare.

Argon began to run, slowly at first but gradually picking up the pace as the great beast began to move.

Then it happened.

Amid a colossal drive to leave its nest, the Maw gave a sudden, lurching shudder and then seemed to fall again, its tentacles scrambling madly on the cavern floor as it receded back into the hole.

It's stuck, Argon thought, suddenly pausing in his mad dash around the cavern perimeter. *That's why it didn't break free after the collapse – it's actually stuck in the hole.*

He was about to relax when the tentacles

suddenly snapped out again, snaking high into the air and whipping around the walls in a mad frenzy.

Argon gasped and leapt aside, just as one of the Maw's giant limbs smashed a hole in the path where he'd been standing. This caused a small rock collapse that, Argon realized, might present some problems when he came around for his second circuit of the cavern.

Bellowing again, even *louder* this time, he continued his breakneck run, skidding to a halt when a second tentacle slammed into the wall ahead of him.

The Maw was evidently becoming extremely frustrated. It twitched, writhed and wriggled helplessly in the ground, its great twisting limbs searching for anything it could grip that would enable it to drag itself up and out of its rocky prison.

Unable to achieve this after several attempts, the beast's movements became more frantic. One tentacle flashed back and forth faster and faster, searching, probing, smashing away great sections of the walls. Then, in a raging torrent of frustration, it opened its massive, needle-filled jaws and roared with such deafening ferocity that the entire cavern shook in a great quake.

As the Maw's mouth widened and stretched to the limits of its physical capability, Decimus appeared from behind a collapsed section of rock on the cavern floor and – to Argon's astonishment – leapt over two of the tentacles as he hurtled *towards* the central mass of the Maw.

Then, taking a giant and apparently suicidal leap, the young gladiator dived directly between the jaws of the beast, disappearing inside it as they snapped shut in a sudden, reactive gulp.

Argon froze, mid-yell, too stunned by the sight even to continue with his friend's plan.

Decimus had been consumed by the Maw . . . and he'd done it *on purpose*.

The army of Slavious Doom climbed Mount Vesuvius in three separate groups. The first, led by the overlord himself and his deceptively agile apprentice, were nearly at the crater. The second group, comprising the main mass of the army, were still a little way behind them. The last group were a good distance away, still dragging the parents of Decimus Rex through the mud and pausing every few hours to punish the pair in small and malicious ways for slowing them down.

As the crater of Vesuvius came into sight, Doom turned to the Mirror Master with a grave expression on his craggy face.

'We will camp on the edge of the crater for a few days, to give our young friend enough time to find and retrieve the sword.'

The Mirror Master shook his head. 'You really think he . . .'

'. . . absolutely. He is *destined* to possess it . . . and when he does – when he and his friends attack – I want you and the men to separate him from the others. Do you understand? I want to fight Decimus Rex *alone*.'

The Mirror Master bowed slightly. 'As you wish, my lord.'

Decimus Rex's friends strongly suspected that he was incapable of feeling *fear*. In fact, the opposite was true: Decimus had been terrified in the face of every opponent, every trap and every danger he had ever faced. The thing that made him look so fearless to his friends was the fact that he had learned to channel all his terror and use it to his own advantage. This occasion was no different: he felt the fear building inside him . . . and began to turn it around.

The incredible, needle-thin jaws of the Maw slammed shut above him and he landed with a

wet plop on something that he just knew,
instinctively, had to be the monster's lolling
tongue. The slimy surface, which convulsed
reactively upon his landing, contained what felt
like hundreds and hundreds of tiny hairs. They
impeded his progress, for as the Maw's tongue
made every effort to flip him into its massive

throat, the hairs were halting his downward slide. Decimus fought them, wrenching his arms and legs away from the carpet of tiny spikes in an attempt to force himself into a further dive for the beast's stomach.

It worked.

Decimus peeled himself away from the huge, lolling tongue and slid vertically down the tunnel of the Maw's pulsating throat. Down he plunged, faster and faster, assisting his passage by keeping his arms and legs tight together.

The horrible tract he found himself in flashed by in a blur, and he plummeted through stinking rotten air for a fraction of a second before splashing into a tumultuous soup like a stone dropped into water. He sank beneath the surface, holding his breath as the tide of putrid liquid rose and fell above him.

Opening his eyes, he could barely see through the murky gloom of the Maw's foul stomach contents. On reflection, this was probably just as well: only the gods knew what such a creature would have devoured before its forced hibernation.

Then he saw the glow. Even in the inky swell of the stomach fluid, the blade shimmered and shone like a candle.

Decimus surfaced once again, took a deep gulp of the wretched air and dived below, propelling himself through the stomach pool and making for the blade with a grim determination.

The Maw was going crazy.

Argon had been forced to hurtle around the cavern ridge at breakneck speed, leaping increasingly bigger and bigger gaps as the beast's raging tentacles blasted more and more of the rocky path away.

Still bellowing with every breath he had left, Argon kept up the pace, feeling his energy beginning to ebb away from him, until finally . . . he collapsed on to his knees. Puffing and panting out great lungfuls of air, Argon could only look on helplessly, as his greatest fears came to life, right before his eyes.

Two of the probing, thrashing tentacles finally found their way to the tunnels at either end of the cavern roof, and snaked inside. After a few, frantic seconds, they pulled taut, dragging the bodily mass of the Maw with far greater intensity.

It took only three great heaves before the beast began to escape. Argon looked on, petrified, as more and more of the gigantic monster's great bulk became visible, squeezing itself from the crack as its great feelers wrenched it upwards.

Then, all at once, the Maw was free.

Tentacles now lifting as well as pulling its enormous frame, the beast scrambled across the cavern floor, convulsing as if caught in some inner struggle. Its jaws snapped back and forth as its eyes searched the area madly for the source of the screaming that had awoken it.

The Maw's nest of emerald eyeballs darted about until they fixed upon the hunched form of Argon, still on his knees atop the ridge pathway.

Moving at a speed that seemed impossible for a creature of such size, the Maw made its way up the cavern walls. Argon could only stare at his approaching nemesis. The beast looked like the giant, mutated offspring of a spider and an octopus as it lashed out a stream of its deadly tentacles.

Argon closed his eyes as the giant feelers came smashing down, and tried to pray to the gods to take him quickly.

There was a terrible rush of air.

The Maw screamed . . . and it *was* a scream. Unlike the terrible, shuddering roar that had rocked the cavern earlier, this high-pitched, wailing cry was akin to the sound a thousand wounded dogs might make if they all howled at the same time. It was absolutely deafening and

Argon, suddenly aware that he was still alive
and breathing, raised two hands to cover his
ears. When a second scream rocked the cavern,
he slowly chanced opening his eyes in order to
see what was happening.

The Maw had fallen from the ridge path, and

was writhing around on the cavern floor, its tentacles flailing madly in the air.

For a second, Argon just stared down at the beast, wide-eyed, completely unsure of exactly what was happening to it.

Then the sword appeared. The fiery, glowing blade erupted from the stomach of the beast in one swift thrust, spewing a fountain of green liquid all over the floor of the cavern.

The blade cut downwards, opening a neat line in the Maw's slimy flesh as it continued to scream. Its tentacles suddenly withdrew as if to scratch an infuriating itch.

Decimus exploded from the belly of the beast, bursting forth on the wave of rank stomach juice that gushed from within.

Sliding across the cavern floor, Decimus

quickly flipped himself over and scrambled on to his feet, just as the Maw made a furious, desperate lunge for him with all eight of its tentacles.

Now screaming with an intensity that put Argon's former cries to shame, the giant feelers whipped around in a series of wild arcs as they prepared for a final, devastating attack.

Decimus had a face like black thunder. Moving to stand on firmer, rockier ground, he crouched in a battle stance, clutching the Blade of Fire in both hands, his eyes narrowed to slits as he watched the movement of every tentacle with acute awareness.

Two of the giant feelers shot out for the attack, but Decimus moved like a flash of lightning. The young gladiator hacked off the end of the first tentacle in one sweeping cut and promptly leapt over the next, only to dash after it and slice the end cleanly away.

Another series of howling screams echoed around the cavern, as streams of the green liquid vaulted from the tips of the wounded feelers. The other tentacles were quickly withdrawn in a wild panic.

Giving the beast no opportunity to regroup for a new attack, Decimus spun the glowing blade around in a full circle and hurtled towards the main body of the Maw.

Watching from the ridge above, Argon felt cold and useless. He just stood, in a state of bewildered awe, as his friend ploughed into the shuddering mass, driving the blade forward in a frenzy of demented thrusts and sending up great sprays of the jade-coloured blood in every direction.

Finally, the Maw gave one last, ear-splitting, ground-shuddering roar of despair ... before its mass visibly deflated. The remaining tentacles flopped lifelessly on the cavern floor and trembled slightly, the movement slowly easing as the life left them.

Decimus staggered back from the enormous mass of the beast and collapsed on to his knees, the sword clattering to his side. As Argon half slipped, half tumbled down the rocky walls of the cavern, Decimus began to wretch as his body threw up the filthy soup he had swallowed in the stinking stomach of the Maw. Despite the horrible sickness and the urge to cleanse his system of the filthy liquid, Decimus allowed himself an exhausted smile.

The first battle was over: the Blade of Fire had finally been retrieved.

'Here he comes.'

Gladius grinned at the approaching shape of Teo, who was dashing along the side of the volcano at such a high speed that even Ruma and Olu couldn't watch without passing a remark on it. The little slave had been sent off to scout out the crater, while the rest of the army rested on the far side of the mountain. It was a good plan to use Teo, who was so stealthy that he could probably have sneaked past even the most keen-eyed observer in *plain sight*.

However, the puzzled look on the little

slave's face didn't exactly fill the others with confidence.

'They make camp,' Teo said, pausing to draw breath as he reached the group. 'Top of mountain; some sleeping now.'

'Why would they put down a camp?' Ruma exclaimed, his eyes searching Gladius's face for any sign of an answer. 'It doesn't make sense.'

'I agree,' added Olu. 'Why not just throw Decimus's parents into the crater if that's what he's come here to do.'

'"If that's what he's come here to do",' Gladius said, repeating the other slave's words almost as if he didn't realize he was speaking aloud. 'But ... but what if killing Decimus's family *isn't* the thing he's come here to do?'

The statement provoked confused expressions

from Olu, Ruma and Teo, but Gladius continued following his own thoughts to their conclusion.

'Don't get me wrong,' he muttered. 'I'm certain Doom means to execute them, but what if that's not his *main* reason for coming here? Remember, he left the arena *before* we defeated the Specials – entrusting them to finish us off completely unobserved. Doom is not usually so careless.'

Ruma and Olu shared a glance. 'So what does that mean exactly?'

'A camp indicates that he's waiting for something,' said Gladius, scratching his head. 'And considering volcanic eruptions are completely unpredictable ... my guess is that he's waiting for us.'

'Us?' Olu gawked at him. 'But that's ridiculous – are you saying that everything we've been through, from escaping the glass fortress and freeing the slaves to this *insane* journey, was *planned* by Doom as a trap?'

Gladius nodded, but it was Ruma who spoke.

'Not a trap for us,' he muttered. 'A trap for Decimus: I suspect Doom thinks Decimus is with us and that we are all still some way behind him. For once, I would disagree with you, Gladius – those men up there are camping because they do *not* expect an immediate attack. For whatever reason, Doom thinks we are all *somewhere else*. That is why I strongly suggest that we strike now, in the cover of darkness . . . and catch them all unaware.'

Gladius thought for a moment, and then

nodded. 'You're right,' he said, pointing to Teo. 'But I think we should we attack with stealth, not frenzy.'

CHAPTER
III

MIDNIGHT
AMBUSH

Decimus raced along the tunnels, holding aloft the Blade of Fire to light his path. The orange glow bathed the passage in a wash of pale light, illuminating the bedraggled form of Argon, who was still exhausted from his mad dash around the cavern.

'Vesuvius is more than a day away,' Decimus shouted, turning right down a new passage that, thankfully, began to slope upwards. 'We'll cut directly across the hills, but we still can't slow

down and make camp until we're at least in sight of the mountain.'

He put his head down and ran on, guided by both the flame and the distant, hopeful prospect of fresh air.

Midnight arrived.

The crater of Mount Vesuvius was smoking, but not because the volcano was about to erupt. The particular flames currently burning all over

the top of the mountain were man-made, as various groups of soldiers gathered around a variety of temporary cooking fires. Many of the men were already asleep, leaving a skeleton crew to take the first shift of the evening.

In one corner of the crater, a team of brutish-looking thugs watched over Decimus's terrified parents, though their attention to the wretched pair didn't extend to offering them any of the food they were cooking.

Near the edge of the crater, Doom and the Mirror Master were locked in some sort of in-depth discussion with three of the army commanders. Occasionally, Doom would mutter something that caused the senior officers to roar with laughter, but it was the enforced merriment of fear rather than any genuine appreciation of the overlord's good humour.

Only the Mirror Master looked distracted from the conversation. The long-haired, noble-faced warrior kept darting concerned glances left and right, peering around the crater as if he was observing some strange, unseen enemy.

Unfortunately for the gathered army, Islaw Danis was looking in the opposite direction when the ambush actually took place.

Far from the sudden, roaring charge that Ruma would have had the slaves make, Gladius's planned attack was quite different.

Some fifty or sixty slaves poured over the perimeter of the crater, creeping in towards the sleeping soldiers on the edge of the camp with careful, deliberate movements. Their swords were drawn silently, and raised with equal discretion as the first wave of slaves crouched beside their unsuspecting foes.

Then, two things happened with such incredible speed that *no single* member of Doom's army had enough time to muster any sort of strong defence.

First, the stealthy invaders slayed the sleeping guards with comparative ease. Secondly, the remaining legion of slaves came charging over the lip of the crater with a combined scream of rage so terrifying that it literally threw the whole of Doom's army into a mad, wild panic.

All over the sides of the crater, armoured soldiers clashed with young slaves dressed in mere rags of cloth. However, the vast physical differences between the boys and their former tormentors were easily outweighed by the ferocity with which they fought: every slave desperately wanted vengeance, while the soldiers merely defended themselves in the same way they would have done against any other enemy. Passion was carrying the battle, and it was swinging every clash in favour of the slave army.

Slavious Doom clambered to his feet, drawing his great sword from its demon-crested scabbard and swinging it around in readiness for the first attack. Beside him, the Mirror Master also leapt up, but he produced not one but two thin swords from a sling-pack across his back, swinging them both in a complicated series of arcs as he moved to his master's side.

However, Doom had frozen to the spot. The overlord's face was a mask of sudden confusion, and he couldn't hide his surprise at the sight of his newly arrived attackers. As his eyes searched the line of foes, he saw no sign of Decimus Rex: none whatsoever.

All he saw before him were the determined faces of Gladius, Olu, Teo and Ruma: the four young friends of his arch enemy screamed a raging battle cry . . . and hurtled towards him. Doom roared his own bellowing threat, and leapt forward to meet them, Danis close at his heels.

Night yawned over the hills west of the arena, as Decimus and Argon camped beside a flickering fire. The Gaul had fallen into a deep sleep, but Decimus knew they couldn't rest for too long. They still had a long way to go.

Suppressing a wide yawn, the young gladiator felt himself begin to nod off, but managed to avoid the ravages of sleep by rubbing his eyelids with his rough fingers.

As he sat by the edge of the fire, silently yawning, his tired gaze briefly settled on the glowing Blade of Fire which was propped against the rock beside him. He reached out to touch the weapon, but his clumsy grasp only caused it to slide off the rock and clatter loudly to the ground.

Decimus looked over at Argon, but the Gaul began to snore, showing no sign that his own rest had been disturbed by the noise.

It was only when Decimus leaned over to retrieve the weapon that he noticed something had been knocked out of place: the pommel was slightly apart from the hilt. He reached out and picked up the sword, turning it upside down in order to get a closer look at the damage.

In fact, it wasn't damage at all. Pulling at the pommel, he discovered a small, concealed space inside the hilt. Working his fingers into the narrow hole, he felt a tiny roll of parchment, and quickly dragged it out of its hiding place.

The parchment looked old beyond any count of years, and almost fell apart as Decimus rolled it open. Slowly, his lips muttering and mumbling as he went, Decimus began to read about the long and terrible history of the weapon he was holding.

When he'd finished reading, the young gladiator's eyes were drawn to the sword. He found his gaze fixed on the pulsating glow of the blade, and his eyes were filled with tears.

The two armies clashed violently all over the crater. Hordes of screaming children, armed with swords and fired up with the determination of revenge, broke against the wall of soldiers like a giant wave crashing over lines of jagged rocks.

However, despite the incredible ferocity of the attack, a single fact remained: the soldiers were trained to fight, and their smaller opponents were not. Without the lion roar of a determined and heroic leader, the youthful army of the tortured and persecuted slaves could only hold back the mass of soldiers and seemed unable to do any significant damage to their opponent's numbers.

The quartet of warriors who should have been leading them were otherwise engaged, wrapped up in a pitched battle of their own on the far side of the crater.

Slavious Doom smirked at Ruma and Gladius as the pair approached him. Maintaining his battle stance, he neither flinched nor averted his gaze when the first sword was thrust forward.

Doom blocked Gladius's clumsy lunge and swung his incredible bulk around to blast Ruma aside before the skinny Etrurian could muster a single strike. Then he blocked a second, more calculated lunge from the big slave, delivering a forearm blow which drove the boy backwards and knocked the wind from his lungs. Two swords clattered on to the ground, only to be snatched up again as the frustrated slaves groped around in panic.

'Pathetic,' Doom growled. 'I needn't have bothered unsheathing my blade.'

Across from him, Islaw Danis was making short work of both Teo and Olu. The smallest, quickest member of the slave group had attacked the Mirror Master head on, relying on his greater stealth to carry him through the combat. Only, as it turned out, Teo didn't *have* greater stealth than the Mirror Master: the long-haired warrior outpaced him at every turn, eventually disarming him and thrusting one of his two blades deep into the small boy's shoulder. Teo cried out, and staggered back, but Olu's attempt to save his friend had an even more disastrous result.

The gangly slave, who had already tried and failed several times to work his own sword through the Mirror Master's incredible defences, made a frantic thrust in order to block Danis's obvious attempt to finish Teo off.

The Mirror Master did something both unpredictable and completely unexpected with his two swords: he threw them into the air. Wrong-footed by the move, Olu inexplicably found his gaze following the trajectory of the blades. When, in the split second that he realized his mistake, he shook himself out of the reverie and drove his own weapon forward, the Mirror Master caught the two swords and twisted them into a sharp cross, snapping Olu's blade in half.

The lanky slave gasped, looked down at his broken sword, and was sent crashing to the ground by single, high kick to the chest.

Olu quickly rolled over on to his stomach, and screamed. In the few seconds it had taken him to move, Islaw Danis was upon him. With a single demonic thrust, he drove the blade into Olu's back, just below the shoulder.

The gangly slave cried out again, and writhed around in agony.

'You are both wounded in the same way,' Danis said, in a calm voice, looking down at the two fallen boys. 'Neither of you will die, but you will be disabled for a short time . . . at least until all your friends have been defeated. Now, please excuse me – I must assist my master.'

Doom was almost disappointed with his opponents. He'd always known that Gladius would be no physical match for him, but he'd expected a good deal more from Ruma. The scrawny Etrurian, whom Doom had always considered second only to Decimus in the combat stakes, was either completely intimidated or exceptionally tired. Doom reflected that it was probably both, yet still he showed no mercy.

Slamming a fist into the side of Gladius's head and kicking the big slave's legs out from under him, he took a few seconds to step back and admire his handiwork, spinning at the last second to block Ruma's incoming sword strike with a single sweep of his own giant blade. The weapons met with a heavy clash, but the Etrurian's sword flew wide, taking him with it.

Doom laughed with undisguised glee as he followed up on the strike.

Ruma hit the ground with a thud, yet managed to keep hold of his sword and immediately struck back, swinging an arc of steel at Doom's legs. The overlord leapt into the air, cleanly evading the thrust, but evidently forgetting about Gladius, who returned at that moment with a punch that actually knocked Doom slightly off guard.

The overlord rallied with incredible speed, however, swinging back with a punch that knocked the big slave unconscious. He landed with a spine-juddering crash on top of Ruma, who physically convulsed on impact.

Doom sprang to his feet, just as his wily apprentice arrived on the scene.

Danis wasted no time at all, dragging Ruma away from the overlord and pummelling him with a series of well-placed blows that left him disoriented and barely conscious.

Doom grinned at the resulting chaos, and stared out across the crater: his men were winning the combat. Many of the soldiers had simply disarmed the young slaves and were toying with them, allowing them to take their best shots before mercilessly slapping them down. Others were more forthright in their attacks, and were beating the children severely.

The attack had failed, and the advantage had been lost.

Decimus and Argon ran on through the early hours, using their renewed energy to close the already shrinking distance between them and the looming volcano.

Argon had found Decimus's story about the discovery of the scroll absolutely enthralling, but to his annoyance the young gladiator hadn't yet revealed what he'd learned by reading it.

'Can you tell me what the scroll said?' he panted.

Decimus puffed out his own breath of air. 'I'd always heard that the Blade of Fire glowed with an "unearthly flame",' he said, pacing himself, 'and that the gods made it as a weapon of power for the strong and the good of the land to wield against evil. Now, however, I've learned the truth – it is a *cursed* weapon ... I don't think anyone alive today really knows that. Doom told me a long time ago that I bore the Mark of the Blade. See, here on my neck,' he indicated, slowing slightly. 'Legend told that the bearer of this mark was destined to retrieve the Blade of Fire. It seems that this is what Doom always wanted me for ... but he can't possibly know what I've just learned about the sword.'

'What exactly have you learned?' Argon asked, trying to keep the fear from his voice as he ran. 'I mean, how *is* the sword cursed?'

Decimus ran in silence for a time.

'The Blade of Fire was made by the god of

war,' he said, eventually. 'It simply brings death and destruction to all those who wield it. The legend in the scroll isn't exactly clear, but it seems that the gods had grown tired of the fighting of men – millions of years of wars and anger and death – so this weapon was a trick on the bloodthirsty. All who seek to kill another with it will die.'

'I think I understand,' Argon spluttered, as he hurried along beside the young gladiator. 'Basically, if you use it to kill, it is *you* who ends up slain.'

'No wonder it was hidden so well,' Decimus finished, grimacing slightly as he ran on. 'It's quite literally a double-edged sword.'

CHAPTER
IV

DOOM

Morning yawned over the mouth of Mount Vesuvius, and the edge of the crater was a ravaged battleground. Although there were no actual corpses littering the ground, some of the young slaves had been beaten so badly that they lay just as still as if they'd been killed.

In one corner, a pile of swords represented the disarming of the slave army, while another was taken up by the mass of soldiers who now gathered eagerly for the spectacle that was about to unfold.

The Mirror Master, his face a mask of amusement, led a small group of soldiers towards a narrow jut of rock that spilled out over the crater. In front of the group, being urged forward by the swords in their backs, were Gladius, Olu, Teo, Ruma and the parents of Decimus Rex.

All six prisoners were driven on to the rock, their expressions ranging from fear to despair. Ruma's determination had left him, Teo and Olu were ravaged and beaten, even Gladius found himself at a loss to think of anything except the terrible fate now awaiting them.

The group reached the very edge of the rock, and Doom held up a hand, halting their progress.

Just a few more minutes, he thought to himself. *I can almost feel the boy approaching. If my plans have worked perfectly, he will have the Blade with him ... and then it will be mine.*

He raised both hands to his mouth and cried out across the crater: 'We are gathered here today, to discover the dark destiny awaiting *any* and *all* who oppose my rule. You slaves, cowering in the dirt before me, be warned: you can follow these foolish children . . . or you can follow me!'

Doom peered around the crater as he spoke, but there was no sign yet of Decimus Rex. Fortunately, he knew just how to kill time before he despatched the boy's parents.

He took a deep breath, and bellowed: 'Send the first one over!'

A series of sidelong glances

quickly informed the group that, of their number, Ruma was closest to the edge.

The wiry Etrurian felt the blade dig into his back, and took two small steps forward. Looking back at the tear-filled faces of his friends seemed to somehow restore his fighting spirit, and Ruma smiled, shouting at the top of his voice: 'Doom! The last time you had your idiots throw me from a great height, I survived!'

The overlord's face spread into a wide grin.

'I doubt you'll manage the same thing this time, you pathetic gnat,' he roared. 'Your days of escaping my wrath are over. Hahahahaha!'

Ruma swallowed, and felt himself begin to shake. Again, the sword bit into the flesh at the small of his back . . . but this time he could think of no brave words to say. He simply nodded goodbye to the friends he loved, and stepped out over the drop.

'DOOOOOOOM!'

The voice resounded so powerfully that Ruma balked, and would have fallen into the volcano had Olu not steadied him.

Slavious Doom looked east, and saw two figures approaching. One was carrying a sword that glowed, even in the harsh light of day. A smile spread across Doom's dark features like treacle.

'Look, men!' the overlord boomed. 'Look and behold: the great Decimus Rex approaches!'

The army, almost as one, turned to view the scene. A short distance from the encampment, Argon suddenly stopped ... but the young gladiator continued to head straight for the rocky ridge that supported Slavious Doom.

'You see what I carry?' Decimus boomed, once again, holding the sword aloft.

Doom tried not to let his glee betray him. 'If it isn't the fabled Blade of Fire!' he yelled. 'Why, you must have wrenched it from the very jaws of the Maw itself!'

Decimus also smiled, but his was a grin of complete determination: a grin in the face of adversity. The expression baffled Gladius, Olu, Ruma and Teo, who could see no reason for the young gladiator to look *quite* so confident. After all, he had a strong blade . . . but he also faced a vast *army* of opponents.

Still, Decimus walked on.

'So what is the deal, my young friend?' Doom oozed. 'The lives of your parents and your friends in exchange for the Blade?'

Out of the corner of his eye, Decimus saw the Mirror Master detach himself from the slave group and begin to move around behind him. His swords were sheathed, but he was holding a chain of some sort.

Perfect.

Decimus grinned again, and stopped dead.

Then he tossed the sword on to the ground in front of him, and lowered himself on to his knees.

'The deal is that I have had enough of all this killing, my lord,' he said, peering up at Doom. 'So I give you this weapon and ask that you spare my life and the lives of my friends and parents in return.'

As gasps flew up from the gathered slaves, a

look of complete puzzlement consumed the overlord's smug face.

Decimus was kneeling before him, and had ripped his ragged shirt apart to reveal a section of his pale, scarred chest.

'I beg for your mercy, Doom,' he cried, an edge to his voice that even Gladius had never heard.

Doom thought for a moment, and then positively beamed with triumph.

Motioning to the Mirror Master to quicken his pace, he climbed down from the ridge and approached the young gladiator, taking extra care to watch the boy as he picked up the sword in both hands.

'I have it!' Doom screamed, practically crying out to the gods. 'At last, the Blade of Fire is mine! Hahaha!'

The Mirror Master moved behind Decimus and briskly looped the chain he was carrying around the boy's neck.

'Just being *sure*, master,' he growled.

Doom was so focused on the sword that he barely noticed the gesture, but he looked up and nodded some small thanks to his apprentice when his gaze finally returned to the boy.

Decimus knelt, awaiting Doom's mercy, his chest bared and his neck wrapped with the chain. He cast a last, hopeful glance at the overlord, and begged for his life.

'Please, Lord Doom, please ... I am sorry for the embarrassment I have caused you. Spare my life, and the lives of all those I love. I beg of you.'

Doom's fiery eyes locked with those of the boy at his mercy, and he smiled humourlessly.

'For all that you have done to me, Decimus Rex,' he growled, 'THIS is the mercy I give you.'

Doom rushed forward, and in a second that seemed to the slaves to last for an hour, drove his sword at the heart of Decimus Rex...

. . .

. . .

... but the boy wasn't there.

Moving with a snap reaction that would have been far beyond even Teo's quickest spring, Decimus twisted his entire body around and flung himself backwards with all his might. The chain around his neck was pulled forward with lightning speed and the sudden, dead weight of the young gladiator's entire body.

The Mirror Master, still clinging desperately to the end of the chain, flew forward like a bird, soaring into the air . . .

. . . just as Doom arced the Blade of Fire down
to where Decimus had been . . .

There was a second of
blurring chaos . . .

. . . and the sword plunged
into the Mirror Master's chest.
Silence.

Islaw Danis looked down, his
jaw dropping, and staggered

slightly. The sword embedded firmly in his chest, he looked up and smiled weakly at his master.

Then he fell.

Doom's face showed no more than a minor irritation as he strode up to his fallen companion in order to wrench free the sword for a second strike at the boy.

Then, all at once, the overlord seemed to feel an itch in his own chest.

Still reaching down for the blade, he put a hand to his armour, and released the front plate.

It clattered to the ground.

Doom looked down.

The slaves started to whoop, roar, and cheer their approval as the blood-red wash began to soak through Doom's tunic.

The overlord looked up, his eyes wild and

frantic, desperately searching for an answer as the life flowed from his veins.

'You want to know WHY?' Decimus shouted. The young gladiator was on his feet once again, and storming towards Doom.

The overlord sank to his knees.

'It's a *cursed* weapon,' the boy cried. 'Cursed to be wielded by men *just* like you: men who follow battle with battle, death with death.'

As Doom grasped the edge of Decimus's tunic and began to lose consciousness, the young gladiator snatched hold of his fallen nemesis and shouted: 'It's what you searched your whole life for, Doom . . . and now you're welcome to it.'

At the very last second, on the volcano crater, surrounded by once fearful minions and all those whom he had enslaved, the great and powerful

Slavious Doom met his fate.

As the evil overlord died, one by one his men dropped their weapons, some edging slowly away and others abandoning their confidence and simply running down the mountain.

Behind them, a roar started up at the crater top. It was a humming, thundering, rampaging cheer of

freedom, and it got louder . . . and louder . . . and louder . . . and, though the voices of the many slaves gathered atop Vesuvius contributed to the vast sea of noise, none were louder and prouder than those of Olu, Ruma, Teo, Argon and Gladius: the freed heroes from the Arena of Doom.

Decimus Rex himself just smiled because he felt that his days of roaring were now *finally* over.

STEP
INTO THE
ARENA

CHARACTER PROFILE
CAPTAIN LICH

NAME: Captain Andrus Lich

FROM: Rome

HEIGHT: 1.9 metres

BODY TYPE: Tall, stooped, rangy

Fact File: Captain Lich has only one arm and a wooden strut in place of his left leg.
Lich is afraid of no one, and while he follows the orders of his superiors, he never treats them with any particular respect. He calls no man his 'master'.
Lich likes to brutalize those under his command, and regularly attacks the junior guards who follow him.

LICH QUIZ: How well do you know Captain Lich? Can you answer the following questions?

1. HOW DOES LICH KNOCK OUT A GUARD WHO BURSTS INTO THE MIRROR MASTER'S THRONE-ROOM?

2. WHAT DOES CAPTAIN LICH CALL THE MIRROR MASTER?

3. WHICH ARM IS CAPTAIN LICH MISSING?

GLADIATOR GAME

THE WALL RACE

In this very quick but exciting game, one player takes on the role of Teo, while the other plays a Roman guard in charge of unlocking the prisoners and letting them fall to their deaths! Can you repeat the heroic actions of the little slave and save the children as he did, or will they be doomed in this game? To play, you will need two dice, a pencil and a piece of paper. Note: this game is difficult to win, as the evil soldier has the advantage!

First, Teo must catch the soldier, who is

272

already a good distance ahead of him. The cliff-face has fifty footholds. You will need to make a note of the scores as they increase! First, roll two dice for the soldier, giving you a score between 2 and 12. The score is how many footholds the soldier has climbed. Then, roll ONE die for Teo, adding 3 to the score because he is so fast!

If Teo reaches the top first (i.e. gets to 50 or above before the soldier), he has successfully grabbed the keys and must now try to escape immediately. However, there is a two in six chance of Teo falling as he attempts to leap on to the chain-line. You must shout out two numbers and then roll the die. If you get any number *other* than the two you shouted, Teo has survived and has rescued the prisoners. If you get one of the numbers you shouted, Teo has fallen to his doom.

If the soldier reaches the keys first, he must quickly unlock the chains. However, there is a slim chance he will fumble and drop the keys! You must shout out one number and then roll the die. If you get any number *other* than the one you shouted, the soldier has been successful and all the children have fallen to their doom. If you get the exact number you shouted, the keys have fallen and you have lost.

GLADIATOR GAME
THE TOURNAMENT!

This is an exciting game that can be played on your own or with friends. It is an elimination tournament, and features many of the characters from the Gladiator Boy saga. You will need two dice, some paper, a pencil, a bag or container and a number of counters or figures to represent each warrior! First, tear up twenty-one equally-sized pieces of paper and write the name of a character and the number you see next to that character (all listed below) on each one. The number represents the character's Life Points score: when this reaches 0, the character has been defeated and is out of the game.

Now, put your twenty-one pieces of paper into a bag. Then, taking care not to look, put your hand into the bag and draw out two names. So, for instance, your first two pieces might be Drin Hain and Slavious Doom – that means these two warriors will fight each other first! Before you conduct any battles, however, make sure you have drawn eight fights (i.e. sixteen pieces of paper). These eight battles represent the first 'round' of your tournament. The winner of each fight goes on to meet the winner of the next one, and so on – until only one gladiator remains! You can find the exact rules of combat over the page!

HOW TO PLAY

The character with the lowest LP score goes first (if level, it's a coin toss), rolling two dice and adding them together for an 'attack' score. The defender also rolls two dice, for a 'defence' score. If the defence is higher than the attack, there is no damage, but if the attack is higher than the defence, the attacker rolls two dice AGAIN – and deducts the score from the defender's life points. Now, it is the defender's turn to attack. This goes on until one character has been reduced to zero.

Enjoy!

LIFE POINTS

Decimus Rex	60	Sturgenus	30
Slavious Doom	60	Tekaro	40
Olu	20	Miriki	40
Mirror Master	30	Aritezu	40
Ruma	30	Akina	40
Captain Lich	20	Mori	10
Teo	20	Falni	10
Drin Hain	30	Tiberius	10
Argon	20	Hrin	10
Groach	50	Boma Derok	20
Gladius	30		

CHARACTER PROFILE
THE MAW

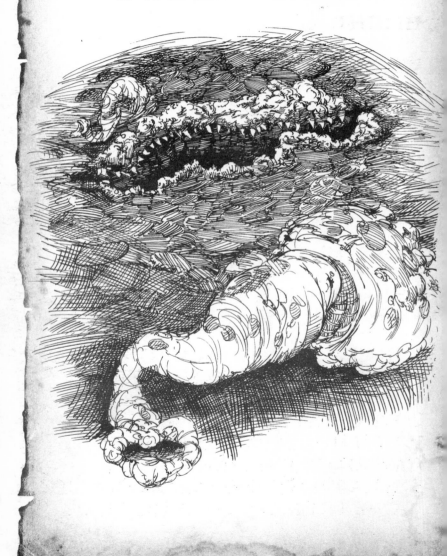

NAME: Unknown (called the Maw)

FROM: The inky depths below Campania

HEIGHT: 6m approx

WEIGHT: 10 tons approx

BODY TYPE: Cephalopod

Fact file: The Maw is thought to be an ancient god of an elder race, left behind when the Earth was abandoned by the original deities who ruled it.

THE MAW QUIZ: How well do you know the Maw? Can you answer the following questions?

1. DECIMUS WENT BACK TO THE MAW IN ORDER TO FETCH SOMETHING. WHAT WAS IT?
2. WHO WAS WITH DECIMUS WITH WHEN HE RETURNED TO THE CAVERN OF THE MAW?
3. WHAT IS IT THAT ARGON DOES TO CAUSE THE MAW GREAT DISTRESS?

Answers: 1. The Blade of Fire 2. Argon 3. Yells/bellows.

Forget everything you've ever seen or heard about werewolves, zombies and vampires because Ed Bagley's going to tell you the single most important fact you'll ever learn: BEING UNDEAD SUCKS ... especially if you're a kid.

Join Ed in this hilarious and freaky series from David Grimstone, featuring a one-armed zombie, a werewolf with a difference and a renegade arm with a mind of its own.

www.undeaded.co.uk

Hod
Child
Boo